Wes put his hand over
"Where's the chapel?"

The fateful words popped out of Wes's mouth without reflection. Raw instinct, like a hawk diving for prey. Time stopped. He heard the jingle and hum of the casino hotel still doing its thing, but the two of them floated alone in a bubble. Veronica's lips were parted. Her brilliant blue eyes were fixed on him, full of confusion.

As well they should be. He was a flirtatious stranger. She should tell him to get lost. He wouldn't blame her. But he'd said what he said. He wouldn't walk it back now.

He wished it was all about her. Veronica Moss's splendor would have been enough to justify what he'd just said. He might have lunged for this chance even if he hadn't been burdened by his agenda. Why not jump up to save the gorgeous damsel? Solve her problems, be her hero and score a killer excuse to be close to her, 24/7. What was there not to love about that scenario?

Just the truth he needed to unearth from the Moss family history.

* * *

Married by Midnight by Shannon McKenna
is part of the Dynasties: Tech Tycoons series.

Dear Reader,

I love a tale about a surprise last-minute wedding set against the glitter and sparkle of Las Vegas!

Now that her cousins are all matched up, it's Ronnie Moss's turn to deal with her aunt's marriage mandate. If she's not married by her thirtieth birthday—tonight—control of the company will be lost. So she plans a Vegas wedding.

But when her fiancé bails on her, she's in big trouble...

Enter the gorgeous Wes Brody, who offers himself up as an alternative husband.

But Wes's family has a dark, painful history with the Mosses. Ronnie can't resist Wes's seductive charm, but his secret agenda weighs on him. Because the more time he spends with Ronnie, the more he wants to give her everything, including his heart...

I hope you enjoy this fourth and final installment of the Dynasties: Tech Tycoons series! I loved writing this quartet. Don't miss book one, *Their Marriage Bargain*, Caleb and Tilda's story, and book two, *The Marriage Mandate*, Maddie and Jack's story. Book three, *How to Marry a Bad Boy*, is Marcus and Eve's story.

Follow me to stay up-to-date! Look for contact links on my website, shannonmckenna.com.

Happy reading!

Warmest wishes,

Shannon McKenna

SHANNON McKENNA

MARRIED BY MIDNIGHT

HARLEQUIN

DESIRE

HARLEQUIN®
DESIRE™

Recycling programs for this product may not exist in your area.

ISBN-13: 978-1-335-58146-4

Married by Midnight

Copyright © 2022 by Shannon McKenna

For questions and comments about the quality of this book, please contact us at CustomerService@Harlequin.com.

Harlequin Enterprises ULC
22 Adelaide St. West, 41st Floor
Toronto, Ontario M5H 4E3, Canada
www.Harlequin.com

Printed in U.S.A.

Shannon McKenna is the *New York Times* and *USA TODAY* bestselling author of over thirty romance novels, ranging from romantic suspense to contemporary romance and even to paranormal. She loves abandoning herself to the magic of a story. Writing her own stories is a dream come true.

She loves to hear from readers. Visit her website, shannonmckenna.com. Find her on Facebook at Facebook.com/authorshannonmckenna, or join her newsletter at shannonmckenna.com/connect.php and look for your welcome gift!

Books by Shannon McKenna

Dynasties: Tech Tycoons

Their Marriage Bargain
The Marriage Mandate
How to Marry a Bad Boy
Married by Midnight

Men of Maddox Hill

His Perfect Fake Engagement
Corner Office Secrets
Tall, Dark and Off Limits

Visit her Author Profile page at Harlequin.com, or shannonmckenna.com, for more titles.

You can also find Shannon McKenna on Facebook, along with other Harlequin Desire authors, at Facebook.com/harlequindesireauthors!

One

There he was again. Mr. Mysterious was giving her that wickedly sexy smile again from across the room.

Who was he? The reception that followed her keynote address was by invitation only. Invitations were for big donors. Ronnie could have sworn she knew all those people, by sight, at least. She would have remembered that guy.

Look away. Breathe. Veronica Moss smiled at the man in front of her and tried to remember what they were talking about. Franklin Dodd was a kindly old gentleman with a wispy white goatee who chaired the board of directors of the Kitsup Foundation, which supported scientific literacy in children. They were talking about policies to support math instruction in early childhood education.

Pay attention. Act intelligent. Look alive. Hard, with

her bandwidth all taken up by the effort it took to not turn and stare.

She'd first seen him from the stage during the keynote speech she'd just delivered at the Future Science Conference in Las Vegas. It had been the challenge of a lifetime to her concentration, but she had not screwed up. Then, during the standing ovation, he'd locked eyes, kissed his fingertips and blown the kiss at her.

She had felt that kiss on every inch of her skin. That terrible flirt.

She managed an intelligible reply about educational policy to Dr. Dodd and turned to wave at a passing acquaintance. He was still smiling, waiting for her to gawk at him again.

Stop this girlish crap. She was a grown woman. She had made her life choices. The biggies, anyway. She and Jareth had obtained their marriage license yesterday at the Clark County Courthouse in Las Vegas. At midnight, she turned thirty, and to keep her promise to her aunt and cousins, she had to be married by then to ensure that MossTech, the huge biotech and agri-tech company founded by her uncle Bertram and her aunt Elaine, did not pass into Jerome's hands.

She had put herself into this mess with her own hands.

Ronnie bitterly regretted the childish impulse that had come over her at her cousin Maddie's wedding. She'd been so angry after Jerome, her dad, tried to ruin the event. He'd been spitting mad ever since Ronnie's aunt Elaine legally mandated that her three grandchildren—Ronnie's first cousins, once removed—be married, Caleb and Marcus by age thirty-five and Maddie by age thirty, or else watch Ronnie's father, their uncle Jerome, take control of MossTech. A dreadful prospect.

Then, on Maddie's wedding day, Jerome somehow hid the papers that had to be signed after the ceremony. Once the clock ticked over to midnight on Maddie's birthday, it would be too late. But Maddie and Jack had gotten secretly married beforehand, just to keep their asses covered. Curses, foiled again.

Then there was that shady stuff her dad pulled on poor Marcus and Eve, setting them up so that it looked like Marcus had betrayed Eve. It was sheer luck for her cousin and his bride that things had gotten ironed out, and trust restored. She'd been so sick of it. Personally, too. Her dad had been harsh and critical ever since she could remember, and the night of Maddie's wedding, her rage had boiled over.

Ronnie hadn't been a part of her aunt's mandate at first, being only a niece. That honor had gone to Aunt Elaine's grandchildren. Her aunt felt guilty for having raised them to be workaholic overachievers, and her solution had been to manipulate the three of them into matrimony by waving the threat of Jerome over their heads. But after her dad's embarrassing performance at Maddie's wedding, Ronnie had begged Aunt Elaine to put her into the documents, too.

At the time, it felt like the perfect way to hurt her father. Deny him something that he actually cared about; i.e., controlling MossTech, wielding power, making money. It wasn't like she could punish him by estranging herself. He wouldn't care, or probably even notice. But this? Oh, this, he would definitely notice.

It took a while to convince Aunt Elaine, but Jerome had given her a terrible scare, so she let Ronnie talk her into it. Same terms. Same punishment if she failed. Controlling shares of MossTech would pass immediately to Jerome. A fate dreaded by all.

Of course, for her, the marriage mandate wasn't as fraught as it had been for her cousins. She was a sure thing, safely engaged to one of the producers of her TV show. Jareth was handsome and smart, extremely competent, personally interested in her career, and wealthy in his own right. She'd been flattered by his offer, though she'd dodged setting a date for months. There always seemed to be some pressing reason to wait a little longer.

Not anymore. She turned thirty on the stroke of midnight, and the mandate had to be honored. Or else.

She'd get a video of the ceremony, held in a cheesy wedding chapel, officiated by the flashiest Elvis impersonator she'd been able to find, and send it to her dad. Ka-pow. The final blow. It was hers to deliver, after all the hell he'd put her through.

Then she'd go no contact forever.

Not that there would be much to miss. Derision and contempt. No tenderness that she could remember.

But she was okay. She'd learned to live without it. God knows, Jareth wasn't the touchy-feely type. He'd been genial and flattering at the beginning, but as the months went by, bit by bit, the flattery had faded away. Jareth was all business. Constantly working, constantly hustling.

But she didn't hold that against him. As a Moss, she had a deep respect for hard work and dedication. It was childish to expect the man to make a constant fuss over her. He'd made her show a huge success, after all. What was good for Jareth was good for her. It really was.

The problem was, after the heat of the moment faded, her gesture toward Dad had started to feel small and spiteful. She could have left things as they were. Dad would still have lost his chance to get control of Moss-Tech, but she wouldn't have been the one to strike the final blow.

Too late for regrets. She had to see this through, like her cousins had done. Spectacularly, too. It had been a last-minute miracle for Caleb, Maddie and Marcus to get married in time. And not just married. They were crazy in love. Over-the-moon happy. All three of them.

It made her feel almost…well, jealous. Left behind.

Which was silly. Jareth Fadden was a perfectly good fiancé. Tonight, he would become her perfectly good husband. Jareth had a lot going for him. He was creative, successful, ambitious, energetic. All qualities she admired. She had no cause to envy anyone.

Dr. Dodd's talkative wife joined him, and over Mrs. Dodd's shoulder, she saw Jareth keeping a sharp eye on her from across the room. As always, checking to make sure she was paying attention to the right people. He was forever scolding her for getting into conversations with people who in his estimation were not worth her precious time.

She gave Jareth a reassuring smile and wave, signaling that she was on top of it.

"Franklin, let's visit the buffet," Mrs. Dodd said. "I'm light-headed from the champagne. I need actual food."

"Of course, my dear." Dr. Dodd gave Ronnie a gallant bow. "Dr. Moss, can I get you a plate from the buffet as well?"

"No, thank you," she said with a smile. "Go on ahead. I'll see you in a moment."

The Dodds linked arms and made their way toward the buffet. Over their heads, she saw Mr. Mysterious take a champagne flute from one of the trays circulated by the catering staff. He raised his glass to her. God, that smile.

Now that he was closer, she saw how tall he really was. He towered over the people around him. His shoulders and chest and face were broad, his jaw strong and square. Intense dark eyes under heavy dark brows. That grin was drop-dead sexy.

She smiled back, and lifted her hand with her engagement ring, fluttering her fingers so that the huge diamond winking there would catch the light and send its clear, sparkling message. *Already taken. Done deal. Sorry.*

Mr. Mysterious's smile turned rueful. He smacked his hand against his heart, as if mortally wounded. Clown. She turned away, spotting another caterer with a tray of glasses going by, and reached for some champagne. She definitely needed to fortify herself.

Bridal jitters. This kind of thing always happened when one made a commitment to any course of action. It was just Fate, tormenting her with the lost possibilities, paths not taken.

She wouldn't let it rattle her. The marriage license was in her purse, with two white gold wedding bands. She'd been wearing Jareth's engagement ring for months now and had the snagged and ruined sweaters and scarves to prove it. The setting of the jutting diamond was pure destructive hell for her cashmere wardrobe pieces, but it was a magnificent stone, and life was a series of trade-offs.

"Hell of a rock you've got there," said a deep voice behind her.

Ronnie spun around. Mr. Mysterious, at dangerously

close range. His aftershave was warm and citrusy and delicious. "Excuse me?"

"Sorry. Was that too personal a comment?" he asked.

"I'm not sure yet," she hedged. "Your wording was ambiguous."

He held out his hand, and she offered her own before she could think better of it. Not an intelligent move, she realized, as his hand enveloped hers. It was warm. His calloused palm felt supple, like seasoned leather, like hand-polished wood.

"Not ambiguous at all," he said. "I was referring to the rock on your ring finger. I have mixed feelings about it."

I am not interested in your feelings about me, my ring, my rock. That was what she knew she should say, but all that came out was a wispy little "Oh."

"I'm sorry to see that ring," he mused. "But I don't see a wedding band."

The nerve of this guy. Ronnie gazed into his smiling dark eyes. "Have we met?"

"No. I'd remember if I'd seen you before in the flesh. I'm Wes Brody." He shook her hand, which he had never relinquished. "I know who you are, of course. The photos in the conference booklet don't do you justice. I'm a big fan, by the way. I've watched every episode of *The Secret Life of Cells*, many times. It's brilliant. And so are you."

Ronnie withdrew her hand, with a tug. "Thanks." She tried to keep her voice cool, but it ended up sounding prim.

"Your presentation was amazing," he said. "I could listen to you forever."

"You're very kind," she said. "I saw you in the audience."

"Yeah. I had a prime seat." His grin widened. "You

don't even want to know the shady stuff I pulled to get a place right at the front."

"No, I really don't," she agreed. "Let it be shrouded forever in secrecy."

"So." He paused. "Could I buy you a drink, afterward?"

Ronnie shook her head. "No. My fiancé and I are getting married this evening."

Wes Brody's eyes widened. "Tonight?"

"Yes. A wedding chapel, an Elvis impersonator who sings while we sign the paperwork, the whole shebang. And I do have a wedding ring. His 'n' hers. In my purse."

"Ronnie!" It was Jareth's voice, with that sharp, dictating tone that made her hairs stand on end.

She could not snap to it in front of Wes Brody.

Brody's eyes narrowed as he gazed over her head. "That's the guy?" he asked. "The one who's bellowing at you right now?"

"That's him," she said. "Well, then. It's a big night for us, so thanks for the—"

Tweeeeet. A deafening whistle split the air. She flinched. Damn, Jareth. Here?

God, how she hated that habit of his. Hated it intensely.

"He *whistles* for your attention?" Wes Brody looked appalled. "He has the freaking nerve? In public, at a reception given in your honor?"

"Not your business." Her face was hot.

"My mother would've had something to say about that," Brody said. "She had clear, articulated ideas about how a man should behave around a lady. I didn't always measure up to her exacting standards, but I tried. I knew what side my bread was buttered on."

"Good for you," she said, inanely.

"Ronnie!" Jareth's voice got louder as he approached. "What is the matter with you? Have you gone deaf?"

Wes Brody leaned closer to her. "Pro tip," he whispered. "Don't marry that guy."

Ronnie looked over her shoulder at Jareth. When she looked back, Wes Brody had melted into the crowd. A neat trick, for a guy his size.

"Ronnie?" Jareth scolded. "You're in a daze! Are you deliberately ignoring me?"

"Do not whistle at me ever again, Jareth," she said. "I am not your dog."

Jareth looked startled. "Whoa! Since when did you get so damn sensitive?"

She set her empty glass onto the tray of a passing caterer and turned back to him. "I always disliked it. I should have told you before. But I'm telling you now."

Jareth lifted his hands. "Okay, okay! Simmer down. I was trying to get your attention, while scrambling like a bastard to serve your interests. Samuel Whitehall invited us to the Observatory tonight, his luxury retreat in the mountains, and he's offering us a ride in his helicopter. Just twenty people are invited, the who's who of our business, and thanks to me, he's interested in *The Secret Life of Cells*! Whitehall could take us to the next level."

Ronnie craned her neck, scanning the room one last time for Wes Brody. She'd met Samuel Whitehall a few times. Not her favorite person. He leered and stared, he made suggestive comments, he was an "accidental" toucher and an enthusiastic shoulder-massager. He was also immensely powerful in the TV world.

But compromises had to be made. Or so Jareth constantly reminded her.

"Who are you looking for?" Jareth asked impatiently. "Did you hear what I said? Are you even connecting, Ron? This is Samuel Whitehall I'm talking about!"

"That's great, but we have other plans tonight, Jareth, remember? Personal plans."

Jareth rolled his eyes. "Ron, Whitehall's bringing us into his inner circle! We cannot blow this event off. It's important for both our careers."

"We're getting married tonight!" she insisted. "This has to happen before I turn thirty! You know that!"

Jareth sighed. "Seriously? This symbolic stunt to piss off your dad is more important to you than the biggest networking opportunity we've ever had?"

"It is extremely important! I've explained it more than once."

"Fine," Jareth said lightly. "It's early yet. We to the Observatory for dinner, and then head back to Vegas and get married. Easy-peasy, problem solved. Let's go. Samuel's waiting in his own personal limo to take us to the helipad."

"Helipad? We won't have any control over the timing if we're dependent on someone else's helicopter! Let's get married first, and then drive to the Observatory. They can toast to our wedding after dinner."

"No," Jareth snapped. "Catching a ride in the helicopter is part of the scene, Ron. It has to be spontaneous. Samuel's parties can get pretty wild." He cast a critical eye over her elegant ivory suit. "I wish you weren't dressed so primly."

Whitehall's parties tended toward the depraved side, which was not her scene. Maybe she was prudish, but in her heart, she was a hopeless science nerd.

"You don't have a spontaneous bone in your body,"

she told him. Ronnie crossed her arms over her chest, chilled. "I know you work hard on my behalf, but when it comes to our plans for tonight, it's simple math, Jareth. If we take a helicopter to Whitehall's party, we won't be back in time to get married."

"Of course we will," Jareth scoffed. "Don't be silly."

"I'll go to Whitehall's party," she said. "But only if we go to the wedding chapel first."

Jareth's reassuring smile faded. "Ron. You're being irrational."

His eyes had a chilly glitter. A sinking realization took form. "You never meant to go through with this to begin with, did you? You organized this, just to have an excuse for getting back too late to get married by midnight."

"Don't be such a drama queen. Everything is not all about you, you, you."

"That wasn't a denial," she said. "So it's true?"

"Goddammit, Ron, that's the wrong question to be asking!"

"Answer it anyway," she persisted.

"All right, fine. If you insist." Jareth leaned forward. "You're too blinded by your anger at your father to keep your own best interests at heart."

"*My* best interests?" she repeated.

"Yes, Ron! Yours, mine, ours! It's my job to put the brakes on this idiocy. I hoped to do it in a way that would feel like it wasn't anyone's fault, but that was too much to hope for. With you, nothing is simple. It has to be a big, fat, complicated production."

"You can't be serious," she said blankly. "You can't do this to me."

"Take the larger view," Jareth urged. "Go to the Observatory with me. Network with me. We're an unbeatable team. Let the deadline pass. Tomorrow, we'll wake up and take stock of our new prospects, which will be brighter than they have ever been before."

"Prospects?" she said.

Jareth sighed. "You're being deliberately obtuse. If Jerome gets those controlling shares, he'll take MossTech public. Ultimately, the payday for you will be phenomenal."

"No! I promised Aunt Elaine! She only put me into the paperwork because I urged her to! And I only did that because you'd already suggested we run off to Vegas and arrange a party later! I thought you were on board with this! You've tried to get me to elope to Vegas more than once!"

"That was before. You hadn't loaded this huge agenda on top of it," Jareth said. "Your aunt is an adult, Ron. Let her take responsibility for her own actions."

"But I gave my word! To her, and to Caleb and Marcus and Maddie!"

Jareth gave her a thin smile. "Maybe you did, Ron. But I sure didn't. I want to marry you, yes. But not on these terms. So let's change the terms."

Ronnie took a step back, on rubbery legs. She had the strange, disorienting feeling, as if a spell had been broken, and she was seeing the real Jareth for the first time. "You've seen what I stand to inherit when we did the prenup," she said. "It's a crap-ton of money. You have plenty of your own to begin with. So why?"

He shrugged. "So why not write a few more zeros on the end of that number?"

"Because it's a betrayal of my family, and I love them!"

"Excuse me for putting our own interests, and our future children's interests first," Jareth said. "I'll marry you, Ronnie. Gladly. Just not before midnight tonight."

"It's tonight or never," she told him.

Jareth shook his head. "Don't play power games with me," he said. "You won't win."

"It's not about power," she replied. "It's about integrity. I can't compromise on that!"

"Then you'll find yourself alone, with nothing but your principles to keep you company. Not even your show. I have final say on renewal for Season Four, remember?"

She sucked in a startled breath. "Really? You'd play that card?"

"Certainly. I'll manage your emotional excesses any way I can, Ron. At this point, I know how to handle you."

"Handle me. Really." Her face burned. "Manage this, Jareth," she said, through her teeth. "Fuck off."

Jareth rolled his eyes. "Oh, come on. We'll talk tomorrow when you've calmed down. You'll thank me later for thinking ahead on your behalf."

"Get away from me," she said.

Jareth pulled out his phone and placed a call. "Walt?" he said into the phone. "Yeah, it's me… I wanted to give you a heads-up. Looks like *The Secret Life of Cells* won't make it into the lineup for next season… Me too… Huge disappointment… Long story. I'll save it for when I'm back. We'll grab a drink. I'm trying to salvage it, but it doesn't look good. Women, am I right? Can't live with 'em, can't shoot 'em… Yeah. We'll be in touch. Later, Walt."

Jareth closed the call. His gaze was triumphant. He made a scissor-snipping gesture with his fingers. "Free and clear, Ron. Your bridges are burned. Your showbiz career is going nowhere without me and Fadden Boyle Productions."

"Tell me one thing." Her voice shook, to her dismay. "Was this all just about money for you?"

Jareth looked annoyed. "Of course it wasn't, Ron. I admire you. You're bright, beautiful, talented, accomplished. You're too volatile and emotional, but I was hoping that you'd grow out of that—"

"You see me as a child?"

"You act like one," he snapped. "Adults consider every angle. If you change your mind about having a husband, or a career, call me after you turn thirty."

He strode away without looking back.

Ronnie stood there. Rooted in place. She wanted to retreat to her room, but her room was the penthouse suite that she shared with Jareth. It was no refuge.

Get another room. Go to the check-in desk, talk to the staff, pull out your credit card. Move through space, dammit. Left foot, right foot.

But she was too disoriented. She stumbled through the hotel lobby, out onto the street. She wandered down the Vegas Strip, dazed and blinking in the blazing sunshine.

She'd never thought that Jareth had MossTech on his radar. She knew that he liked money and did not mind the fact that her family had it. But forcing her to betray Aunt Elaine and her cousins?

When they first got involved, she'd liked that Jareth was rich. That had been very reassuring, since she'd been beating off would-be suitors who were sniffing after the MossTech billions since she was an adolescent. When she met Jareth, he'd been a driven TV studio executive, in a field light-years distant from biotechnology and agriculture. He barely noticed what her family's company did, what it was worth. He'd been far more interested in how he could monetize Ronnie's own talents. But it had all been an act.

She'd destroyed the only family she cared about, and for what? A chance to spite her father. Score a point. Like a spoiled, stupid child. Jareth was absolutely right about that much, and she was ashamed of herself.

She turned thirty at midnight. No stopping the clock. She'd made a horrible mistake. Jerked around like a puppet by anger and spite, kind of like someone else she knew. The apple didn't fall far from the tree. Maybe that was what she had to look forward to. Her father's life. Poisoned by bitterness and rage. Estranged from everyone, even his own child. The world despised him. What a prospect for her future.

But at least she wouldn't be married to that lying, conniving bastard, Jareth.

Tears overtook her. Jareth hadn't been perfect, and she'd been well aware that he was too domineering, but she'd thought she could manage it. Hah.

One of the big casino hotels loomed over her, blocking the Vegas sunshine, so she went inside, wandering through slot machines. She sat in the quietest bar she could find and ordered a lemon drop, huddling behind her hair as she sipped it.

"Excuse me," said a deep, velvety voice. "May I join you?"

Ronnie froze for several seconds, her heart thudding madly, before she turned.

Yes. The face that went with that gorgeous voice. Mr. Mysterious. Wes Brody.

"It's you," she said.

His smoldering, dimpled smile flashed. "Yeah, last I checked."

She studied him for a moment. "Are you following me?"

"I'm not tailing you from place to place like a maniac, if that's what you mean," he said. "I saw you walk in here, and I followed you inside. I don't mean to be creepy. Or make you uncomfortable in any way."

Ronnie was too numb to register discomfort, or creepiness. "It's okay," she said.

Brody studied her for a moment. "Are you all right?"

"No," she said. "I'm wrecked."

"Does this have to do with the guy I saw? The colossal butthead who whistles for you? Did you fight with him?"

"Big understatement," she said. "We had a catastrophic difference of opinion."

"I see. I know that this is none of my business, and that it's a bad time to chat you up. But if you'd like to talk, I'm all ears."

"Not smart," she said. "I will not sparkle. In fact, I'll probably snivel."

"Warning duly noted, but your misery doesn't scare me. What did that son of a bitch do to you? Want me to flatten him for you? I'm up for it."

"Never mind him," she said. "It's a long, weird story."

"If you tell it to me, will you be late to your own wedding?"

"No," she said. "The wedding is off. Forever."

His eyes lit up. "Damn, Dr. Moss. That's the best news I've had in a long time."

She couldn't stop laughing. "Call me Ronnie. It's terrible news. For me, anyway."

"Then call me Wes, and why is it terrible news? I

think it's awesome. I could tell across a crowded room that guy was a massive jerk. You're well rid of him."

"Maybe so, but I had to get married today," she admitted. "Or else screw up the lives and careers of the people I care about the most. And now it's too late to fix it." Her face dissolved. "And I did it out of spite. I can't believe myself."

Wes pulled a pack of tissues from his pocket. He tucked one in her hand and laid the rest of the pack on the bar. "Sounds like a hell of a story," he said. "I'd love to hear it."

Ronnie blew her nose, mortified. His eyes looked so warm. Sympathetic, fascinated. Not judging. "Really?" she said. "This story does not reflect well on me at all."

"I'm as curious as hell," he said. "May I sit?"

She nodded. Wes sat next to her, and signaled the bartender, pointing at her drink. "Two more," he called out. He spun on the stool to face her. "So? Tell me everything."

"It starts with my dad alienating everyone in my entire family," she began.

It took a few rambling false starts, but Wes's questions were intelligent, and the wheels were liberally greased by two more lemon drops. The story soon poured out of her.

"Anyhow," she concluded. "That's it. In a nutshell, I really love my aunt, and my cousins are like siblings to me. And I screwed them over and let my dad win."

"Ouch," Wes murmured. "Harsh. But I don't get why you asked your aunt to include you in this mandate to begin with. What did you stand to gain?"

"Nothing," Ronnie said bleakly. "Not a goddamn thing. I did it out of spite. I wanted it to be personal. I wanted him to know that when he had his prize snatched away from him, that I was the one who had done it." She winced. "Ouch. Not my finest moment."

"But besides that," Wes mused. "Seems like a huge risk, just for a jab at Dad."

"That's the thing," she wailed. "I didn't think it was a risk! I thought I was safe! I thought Jareth and I were solid. He'd tried to get me to elope before, so I knew he was fine with a Vegas wedding. It never occurred to me that he'd crunch the numbers and decide to screw me over." She paused. "Which makes me not only spiteful, but gullible, too."

"We've all miscalculated a time or two when it comes to love," Wes said.

"Yes, I know, but other people will pay the price for my miscalculation," Ronnie said. "Which horrifies me. And there's absolutely nothing I can do."

"So you turn thirty on the stroke of midnight," Wes mused. "Does this mandate stipulate that your marriage has to be specifically to the whistling butthead? Or would the conditions be met if you married someone else?"

The question threw her. "Ah…I suppose anyone would do. But I turn thirty in a few hours, Wes. It's a little late to go husband hunting."

Wes put his hand over hers. "I'll marry you," he said. "Where's the chapel?"

Two

The fateful words popped out of Wes's mouth without the benefit of reflection. Raw instinct, like a hawk diving for prey. Time stopped. He heard the jingle and hum of the casino hotel doing its thing, but the two of them floated alone in a bubble. Veronica's lips were parted. Her brilliant blue eyes were fixed on him, full of confusion.

As well they should be. He was a flirtatious stranger. She should tell him to get lost. He wouldn't blame her. But he'd said what he said. He'd wouldn't walk it back now.

One part of him was electrified by what this might mean for his secret investigation. The other was just electrified by Veronica Moss herself.

He wished it were all about her. Her splendor would have been enough to justify what he'd just said. He might have lunged for this chance even if he hadn't been burdened by his agenda. Why not jump up to save the gorgeous damsel? Solve her problems, be her hero and score a killer excuse to be close to her, 24/7. Close enough to smell her shampoo. What was there not to love about that scenario?

Just the truth he had to unearth from the Moss family history. About what had really happened twenty-three years ago, at that lab in Sri Lanka, and who was ultimately responsible for the lives that had been destroyed there.

One step at a time, though. Veronica was already traumatized from being used, manipulated and lied to. This enterprise was going to be tricky, and damn distracting, with his racing heart and his glands on overdrive.

God, she was beautiful. He'd admired her on her hit TV show about cell biology, but he'd assumed she'd been helped into that state of perfection by a team of professional makeup artists. But she needed no help. It was all her: dewy skin, delicate bone structure, sharp cheekbones. Rosy, sensual, kissable lips. Huge, startling blue eyes, smudged with mascara. That cascade of tousled, fiery hair. Her body, too. Slim, luscious. A dancer's posture. The whole package: beauty, intelligence, charisma. He'd started watching her show because he was obsessed with the Mosses, but soon he watched it just for her.

What better way to gain her trust? Earning her gratitude? He was being tongue-kissed by Fate…if he could land this opportunity. A very big *if*.

She didn't look trusting or grateful right now. She looked scared.

He wished he weren't so conflicted about it. A functioning conscience was an inconvenient burden.

"Not a good joke, Wes," Ronnie said.

"I'm not joking," he said.

"Of course you are. I don't know you, and you don't know me."

"Maybe not, but with me, you'd be doing better than that last guy," he offered. "I would never whistle for you. I would treat you like a queen. A goddess, even. The utmost respect."

Her eyebrows climbed. "You're not very subtle."

"You don't have time for subtlety," he pointed out. "You told me that your male cousins arranged business marriages to satisfy the mandate. How is this any different?"

"Caleb knew the woman he was getting married to from years before. Marcus picked out someone who had been vetted and cross-checked. They knew both of those women far longer than…how long has it been? Less than an hour, over drinks in a casino bar?"

Wes shrugged. "I don't think your cousins had the same time crunch," he said. "With me, you can save your family company, keep your word to your aunt, keep faith with your cousins, put the shaft to your scheming dad, protect MossTech jobs, and also, incidentally, flip the bird to your venal, butthead ex. All in one smooth gesture."

He realized, with a thrill of excitement, that she was actually considering it.

"Too dangerous," she said. "You know too much about MossTech. I just spilled my guts to you. I don't have a prenup to protect me. I don't even know if your name is really Wes Brody. I don't know you, and I don't know anyone who knows you. You're a smooth talker, but you could be a con artist, or a bank robber. Or a serial killer, for all I know."

He laughed out loud. "I'm not a serial killer. But I'm happy to address your concerns. It's true, I know that you're rich, but I don't care because I'm also rich."

"News flash," she said ruefully. "That was what I thought about the last guy, too."

"I'm not like Jareth," Wes said. "If I want more money, I'll make more money. I'll show you my company website, my tax returns, my stock portfolio. I have my laptop."

"Really," she murmured.

He pulled his wallet from the inside pocket of his suit coat and pried his driver's license out of its slot. "There," he said, presenting it to her. "See? That's me."

She studied it. "Weston Robert Brody," she said. "Nice picture. New York?"

"Sometimes," he said. "I have a house in Manhattan, in Chelsea. I also have a place in Montana. I recently bought a villa on a cliff over the Amalfi coast. I have to get it renovated, but it's got beautiful stonework. It's got a tile terrace overlooking the sea, and lemon trees. I'm always knocking big, juicy lemons off the trees with my head."

"Sounds luxurious," she murmured. "I love lemons. Do you have pictures?"

"Hundreds of them," he assured them. "On my phone. I'll even show you the deed. It's in Italian, but we could find someone to translate it."

"A driver's license can be faked," Ronnie said.

The gleam in her eye hinted that she was messing with him. "I have a passport in the safe in my room. A passport is hard to fake. I'll show you my tax returns, the deed, my investment portfolio. Come up to my room."

"Oh yeah? Will you show me your etchings?"

He grinned. "I'll show you any damn thing you want. Here." He pulled a laptop out of his briefcase and opened it, pulling up the home page of Brody Venture Capitalists. "I own a venture capital company," he told her. "I employ over a hundred people. That's me. Weston Brody, owner and CEO."

She glanced at the masthead photo, then at him. "Impressive."

"No criminal record," he said. "No secrets. Deep pockets. I got an MBA at Harvard Business, and started as an equity research analyst specializing in biotech. I've left a huge digital footprint. Here's the page with some of the start-ups I funded. Any of the people I partnered with would vouch for me. Do you know any of these names?"

She studied it for a moment. "Yes, I do, actually."

"Excellent. Make some calls, or have your people make them. Ask any of the people on that list if I came through for them. I'll wait."

She looked away from him for a moment, biting her lip. "Wes," she began. "Your intensity is gratifying. I appreciate the bona fides. But what do you get out of it? My cousins made bargains that gave a benefit to both parties. But if what you say is true, then you're rich, well-known, successful in your field. You don't need me. So why do such a random, risky thing? What do you get out of it?"

He laughed to hide the discomfort. "Come on," he said. "If you have to ask."

"No," she said. "I absolutely do have to ask. You are an incorrigible flirt. I'm sorry to say this out loud, but it has to be said. Any marriage of convenience that I might

undertake would never presuppose my sexual availability. Never, ever. Got it?"

He gave her a courtly bow. "God, no. The very idea."

"This is serious, Wes."

"I'm not taking this lightly," he said. "But I'm trained
to recognize opportunity. If I feel it, I go with it. I'm not
infallible. I've made some bad calls. But my track record
does not suck. When I see a once-in-a-lifetime opportunity, I don't hesitate. I grab it."

Ronnie's mouth trembled. "I don't feel like such a
stellar opportunity right now," she said. "I feel like a hot
mess. If I were you, I'd back away slowly."

"Not a chance in hell," he said. "Full steam ahead."

She looked away. "Well," she said. "Thank you, Wes.
For the vote of confidence."

"So? Are you going to call your people?"

She blinked at him, sniffing into the tissue. "Call
who?"

"You know, the lawyers, the accountants, the private
detectives. Get the process started. The background
check, et cetera. And there's the small matter of a marriage license." He gave her an encouraging grin. "If I
check out, of course."

"I have a marriage license, but it has Jareth's name
on it," she said.

Wes glanced at his watch. "We have some time yet.
Your people can work on the background check and the
rest while we go to the courthouse and get ourselves a
fresh license. Good thing your amazing keynote address
was a morning event."

"But it's not that simple. I had a detailed, ironclad prenup with Jareth. I can't do a fresh one on the fly, without

the help of my lawyers. It would never be valid in court, and I can't marry you without one."

"We'll do a new one," he suggested. "Let's find an online notary. Get your people to draft something simple. My assets are mine, and yours are yours, unless we feel like legally changing that in a postnup. We'll video-record the whole thing. Your people can send us the forms to sign. We do an online interview, sign it in real time in our recorded video call. Witnessed, signed, stamped, notarized. It's doable, Ronnie."

Ronnie shook her head. "You are a piece of work."

"I want you to have hard proof that I am for real, and not on the grift."

She gazed at him with searching eyes. He returned her look without flinching.

"You know what the problem is, Wes?" she asked slowly. "Why I'm so uneasy?"

"Tell me," he said swiftly. "So I can fix it."

Her lips twitched. "I'm the only one who needs something," she said. "The power balance is off. The stakes are higher for me than for you. That makes me nervous."

"There's no power play going on," he assured her. "I'm fascinated. I'm excited. I'm entertained. For me, that's reason enough."

"It's dead serious for me," she said. "Not entertainment."

"I'm useful to you, even if I'm entertaining myself, aren't I? I'm fulfilling the terms of your aunt's mandate. Whose business is it but ours if I enjoy myself in the process? Who am I hurting by being titillated?"

She rolled her eyes with a snort. "There you go again. And speaking of hurt. You don't have a string of disgruntled lovers who will get their feelings bruised, do you?"

"I'm free as a bird. My parents are both gone, so there isn't even anyone to feel hurt that they weren't invited. No strings. Just a new friend, holding out a helping hand in a time of need." He extended his hand. "So take it."

Another breathless, charged silence. Seconds of frozen waiting…

Ronnie reached out, clasping his hand.

Joyful excitement blazed through him. Discomfort in equal measure, for everything that he hadn't told her. Lying was not the way you treated a queen.

But in his case, lies were a brutal necessity.

"It would be temporary," Ronnie told him. "If the background check comes back okay. I would need you to stay married to me for five years to satisfy the terms of the mandate. Would that be acceptable?"

"I can do five years," he said promptly.

"Of course, you can do anything you like in your personal life, as long as you make the marriage look good for the duration of that term."

"Sounds doable," he said.

"So…really? This isn't a joke, or a trick? You're willing to do this?"

"Really. Go on, make the calls. Do the checks. Have your lawyer draft the prenup. Give me your lawyer's email address, and I'll send him my stuff. Tax returns, investment accounts. Anything he wants to see."

Ronnie pulled out her phone. "What's your number?"

He read it out, waiting while she tapped it into her phone. His own phone chimed with a text.

"My lawyer's email," Ronnie said. "Now you have my number."

He set his laptop on the bar. "I'll send stuff while you make the calls. Then you pick out an online notary and set up the appointment. We better get cracking, or we won't get to the courthouse during business hours."

"Okay," she said. "Excuse me, then."

She retreated to the other end of the bar to make her phone calls. He kept a close eye on her as he sorted through files for documents to send to her lawyer's address.

Ronnie appeared to be having an impassioned argument with someone on the other end of the line. Evidently, her lawyer thought that marrying a random stranger she'd met in a Las Vegas casino bar was a shitty idea. Uptight bastard had no sense of humor.

He wished he had no secrets to hide, because he had absolutely nothing against that radiant creature. He never wanted to hurt her. Veronica Moss deserved reverent awe from every unworthy guy who dared to raise his eyes to her. And even if the Mosses were guilty of the crimes he suspected, the new generation who ran MossTech now was blameless. What their parents and grandparents had done wasn't their fault.

And yet, he couldn't let it go. Because the Moss family had achieved its outsize success at his dad's expense. Wes's father had paid the tab for that family's meteoric rise.

He'd paid for it with his life.

Three

As Fate would have it, the woman who helped them at the Clark County Courthouse was the same one who had generated a wedding license for Ronnie and Jareth the day before. She was a round, stern-mouthed lady with rhinestone-studded glasses. She looked at Ronnie, looked again and looked at Wes. Her eyes narrowed in puzzlement.

"Weren't you in here yesterday?" she said suspiciously.

Ronnie steeled herself. "That's right."

"But not with him." The red-haired lady scowled at Wes.

"Nope," Wes said. "Different guy. A much better one. If I do say so myself."

"Humph." The woman's eyes slid to Ronnie, brows

climbing as she waited for an explanation. Which she was not owed, dammit. It was none of her business.

"It didn't work out with the other guy," Ronnie finally said.

"I see." The redhead clucked her tongue. "That was quick."

"Pretty much," Ronnie agreed.

The woman harrumphed. "Well, I've seen it all, believe me, but I think you beat my personal record for waffling. Maybe you should think this through, miss. Marriage is not entertainment. Ask any married couple. They'll tell you. And it does appear that you two have been drinking. Just sayin'."

Ronnie drew herself up to full height. "I didn't ask for your—"

"Hell, no!" Wes cut her off. "After all the trouble I went to, prying her away from that mouth-breathing troll? She and I were meant to be together. Don't wreck this for me, ma'am. True love stands before you. Please, don't get in its way. It's bad luck."

The redhead snorted. "You do seem more enthusiastic than the last guy, I'll give you that," she said, turning to her keyboard. "I'd call it a step up."

Ronnie couldn't argue with that, though she did not appreciate the commentary. In fact, Jareth had balked, up to the last minute. He'd tried to persuade her that she'd regret not opting for a big wedding. No flowers or photos, no feast, no cake, no fabulous dress, no emotional ceremony, no memories to treasure.

When she held firm, he'd finally signed the paperwork, muttering something about having his balls squeezed in a vise.

Wes Brody did not look like a man who felt that his

balls were being squeezed in a vise at the thought of marrying her. He looked like he'd scored a huge win.

They walked out of the courthouse with the fresh license safely tucked into her purse. She pulled off Jareth's showy engagement ring with an effort and tucked it into her purse, and took out the old marriage license. She tore it into several pieces, flinging them into a recycling bin.

"That looked cathartic," Wes said.

"Absolutely," she agreed. "Good riddance."

"Amen. So have your people checked me out?"

"Yes," she said. "My accountant, my lawyers, the PI firm. A team of experts have been poring over your life. You look great on paper."

"Ah," he said, smiling. "Nice to know."

"It makes them crazy, that they can't find anything bad. You're rich, successful and on the level, as far as they can tell. Your VC company makes money hand over fist. Your luxury properties in Montana, Manhattan and Amalfi are all on public record. The only bad thing that can be said about you is that you're hedonistic. You deny yourself nothing. Gossip magazines babble about your wardrobe, cars, motorcycles, high-profile romantic liaisons—"

"I haven't had any of those in a while," he cut in.

"Poor Joseph made so many phone calls, trying to find someone who would say that you're a liar and a loser, but nobody would oblige him," she said.

"Excellent. So? We've done the bona fides, we've got the license, we have the prenup notarized. What else is holding us back? Shall we go to the chapel?"

"What about me?" she asked. "Did you check me out? It seems only fair."

"Certainly I did." His voice was silky. "At great length. With great pleasure."

"Oh, stop it," she scolded. "I mean, seriously."

"No need," he said. "You're a celebrity, and Moss-Tech itself is the corporate version of a celebrity. You're a household word."

"Oh, please. I'm hardly a household word. Unfortunately, my people are in an anxious tizzy."

"I don't blame them. They don't want to see a rare gem cast before swine. I approve of their zeal and concern." He lifted her hand, and bent over it, in a graceful, ceremonial bow. "And though they can't hear me say it, I solemnly promise to treat you with gentleness and respect." He pressed a kiss to her knuckles.

Her throat clenched. She let her hair fall forward as he held the limo door open for her. She got in, surreptitiously brushing the tears away. This was ridiculous. She was so damn needy, after a lifetime of Jerome's criticism and indifference, and now Jareth's betrayal, too. She was so hungry for the slightest kindness, all Wes had to do was be gallant and nice. Just baseline politeness, and she melted into mush. *Oh yes, please, please, be nice to me, please.*

That made her terribly vulnerable to predators. No wonder Myra and Sam and Joe were so worried. They knew Jerome and Jareth. It was probably written all over her, how compromised she was. Predators could smell that.

Then Wes Brody slid into the limo beside her, his big, powerful thigh just inches from her silk-clad leg. His big hand clasped hers, and the contact sent a deep, beautiful thrill rippling through her. That smile. Those eyes.

His admiration might be an act, but what an amazing act it was. Too pleasurable to resist. In her life, such thrills were not thick on the ground.

Screw it. She'd done what she could to protect herself, legally and financially. She'd survive a worst-case scenario. If he proved to be on the take, at least Aunt Elaine and her cousins were safe and protected. She'd just forgive herself right now, in advance, for all the humiliation and legal hassle that would ensue.

And in the meantime, she'd enjoy the warmth of the contact with him, glowing against her hand. His delicious, focused attention. His charming conversation.

Tonight, Wes Brody was her best bet—and she was betting it all on him.

Wes was glad to see Kenji, his personal assistant, waiting for them outside the wedding chapel, as Wes had directed. Kenji held a box in one hand and an armful of flowers in the other. The younger man's dark eyes were curious as the limo pulled up.

When Ronnie got out of the limo, Kenji gave her a once-over and glanced at Wes, impressed. "Not bad, boss," he said under his breath.

"Didn't ask you, but yeah, I know. Did you take care of the things we discussed?"

"Yeah," Kenji said. "All arranged." He handed over the small box to Wes.

"Excellent." He turned to Ronnie. "This is my personal assistant, Kenji Miyota," he told her. "Kenji, Dr. Veronica Moss. My bride-to-be."

Kenji shook her hand. "I'm a huge fan, Dr. Moss. I've seen that episode about photosynthesis six times. Every time my mind is just…" He mimed an explosion around his head. "You make me feel like I actually understand all the science stuff."

"Aww. How sweet of you. Great to meet you, Kenji. Call me Ronnie." Her smile dazzled Kenji, who kept helplessly shaking her hand.

"Ronnie, could you try this on?" Wes opened up the box, and pulled out the wedding ring he'd asked Kenji to get, hoping to God it would fit. He'd just eyeballed her slender hand, and taken a guess at her ring size.

"But I already had rings!" she protested.

"I didn't want to use them," he said. "Seems unlucky. Wearing a ring bought for the whistling butthead? No, thank you." He handed her the ring.

She slid on the glowing golden band and held out her hand. "It fits perfectly," she said softly.

"Excellent." Their eyes locked, and his heart started to thud. "I'll…um…take that back, then. For the ceremony."

She passed it back, smiling. Wes cleared his throat. "What else have you got for her, Kenji?"

"Ah, yeah. These are for you." Kenji took the wrapping paper off the flowers and presented her with the bouquet that Wes had specified. White calla lilies, orange orchids, floating in an ethereal cloud of baby's breath. Perfect with her red hair.

Ronnie looked startled and touched. "How gorgeous! You didn't have to, Wes!"

"All brides should have flowers. And there's this." He indicated the big box.

Kenji opened it, and Ronnie's mouth fell open as Wes lifted out a beautiful, filmy, lace-trimmed bridal veil, attached to a wreath of fresh rosebuds. The fine, sheer fabric billowed in the faint evening breeze.

"Oh, wow," she whispered.

Wes crowned her with the wreath, draping the veil around her shoulders. This was no job for a future husband. That honor should have gone to her mother, or another significant female relative. But Fate had decreed that Ronnie face this strange milestone alone, with a stranger, on a busy, noisy street in front of a wedding chapel. She looked like a fairy princess. No, actually. She looked like a goddamn angel.

"Wes," she whispered. "That's sweet. I...I don't know what to say."

Neither did he, which was not normal for him. He always had a line for any occasion. But he was struck dumb by awe and dread. A looming sense that he was misusing something that he'd only just realized was precious. Even sacred.

"Ah...yeah," he muttered, strangely flustered. "Kenji, take some pictures. Her alone, and then the two of us together."

Kenji took dozens of pictures of them on the steps, the brilliant colored lights of Vegas behind them. "I'll take pictures inside, during the ceremony if you want," Kenji offered. "Or video the whole thing. You tell me."

Wes looked at Ronnie. "Didn't you want to video this? To send to your dad?"

"Oh, no. I'm embarrassed I ever planned to do anything so mean-spirited. At this point, I just want to forget that part of it. If I'm lucky, my dad never has to know how spiteful I intended to be."

"Ah. So the thing about doing it right before midnight—that's off the table now? We have some time. We could stall for a while, if you wanted. Get a drink."

She checked the time. "If I wait, with my luck, you'd get struck by lightning right before we go into the chapel."

Wes swallowed his laughter. "I'll try to stay alive until then," he said. "No lightning bolts until the papers are signed, I promise."

She laughed nervously. "Sorry."

"Why delay? The sooner we tie the knot, the sooner you can relax." He turned to Kenji. "Just take pictures of the ceremony. And send me the ones you have already."

Wes scrolled through the gallery of Kenji's shots as they walked into the chapel. They were great. Ronnie Moss was photogenic as hell. The floral wreath and veil and the flowers in her arms made her look fey, magical. The veil looked perfect with the starkly elegant white pantsuit. The goddess of spring, in spike-heeled pumps.

But his face looked afraid. Probably he was the only one who could see it. On the surface, he was smiling, confident. But in his eyes, he saw fear.

He didn't want to use her or disappoint her. He wanted to be worthy of her.

But he had to be worthy of his own father, too.

His dilemma began three years ago, when he put the house that his father had owned in Colombo, Sri Lanka, up for sale. The people who had been renting it for the last seventeen years had moved back to London, so he'd decided it was time to simplify. Let go of the past.

Then the agent handling the sale told him about boxes of old papers that had been hidden behind some furniture in a wall closet, forgotten for twenty-three years. Wes had been traveling in Asia at the time, so he'd flown down to Colombo to check it out.

That was where he found his father's journal, and the lab notes, describing an outbreak of toxic mold in a strain of MossTech drought-resistant millet. It had sickened and killed sixty-two people, twenty-eight of whom had been children.

According to his dad's journal, someone had been aggressively covering up the disaster, trying to make the whole thing go away with bribes and intimidation. His father had suspected Naomi Moss, Ronnie's mother, and the rest of the Mosses as well. The data looked bad. In spite of his dad's dry, laconic writing style, Wes could tell how unsettled Dad had felt.

The last journal entry was dated the day of the bombing, twenty-three years ago. John Padraig, his stepfather, had a meeting with Naomi that day. He wrote that she thought someone was following her, and she'd sent home copies of all the documentation, just in case. She'd promised to tell him everything she knew.

That was the day they both died. A bomb had destroyed the lab complex where they were meeting. After, when the toxic mold and the cover-up came to light, it had been pinned on Wes's father. Who had been conveniently dead. Unable to defend himself.

It had broken Mom's heart. First losing him like that, and then having him maligned and falsely accused. Mom had fought for years to clear his name. She'd given up in exhaustion, and died soon afterward.

The journal and the file were the weapons his dad could have used to clear himself, if he'd lived. Now it fell to Wes to follow through. He had to keep all of that firmly in mind. Particularly when Ronnie Moss was making his pulse race.

The Elvis waiting for them was chubby and florid, eyebrows penciled heavily in, sweat beading his forehead from the synthetic white sequined pantsuit. He had a deep, plummy voice with a Tennessee accent, and he smelled of Old Spice and bourbon.

Proceedings got underway. The ceremony was campy and kitsch, but Wes did not feel like he was participating in a joke. He felt like wire with the casing stripped.

He realized that Elvis was asking him to recite his vows. "Excuse me?"

Elvis rolled his eyes. "Do you, Weston Robert Brody, take this woman, Veronica Maud Moss, as your wedded wife, to have and to hold, from this day forward, for as long as you both shall live?" he repeated.

Ronnie had legally specified five years, not a lifetime, but for a brief second, he hesitated to lie to the guy, even though Ronnie had specifically asked him to do so. As if perjuring himself might bring bad luck.

He shook the emotion off by sheer force, and got back to business. "I do," he said.

Ronnie exhaled, giving him a relieved smile, while Elvis turned to her and recited the vows again.

"I do," she responded softly.

"I now pronounce you husband and wife!" Elvis announced. "You may now kiss the bride!"

Wes froze. They hadn't discussed the kiss, and he wasn't making any assumptions with this woman, whose hand he scarcely felt worthy to touch.

Elvis looked impatient. He made a get-on-with-it gesture with his heavily beringed hand.

Ronnie took matters into her own hands. She wound her arms around his neck, pulled his head to her face and kissed him.

Everything lit up when their lips touched. Everything he thought he was sure of was instantly called into question. Everything he believed was impossible might turn out to be real after all. Magic and mystery, bring it on. Anything was possible. Bring on Santa and the Easter Bunny, what the hell. He'd make room. There was infinite room inside him. He could see all the way to forever.

God, her lips were soft. Sweet. Her body felt pliant, hot and vibrant against his, head tilting back, the silky fall of her hair draping over his wrist where he clamped the small of her back, his fingers digging into the fine ivory silk of her suit coat.

He could kiss her forever. Feel the sensation of her high breasts, pressing against his chest, her mouth opening. That low, startled, questioning sound she made—

Elvis cleared his throat loudly. They swayed apart. Her face was red, lips parted. Her mascara-smudged eyes were full of complicated emotions.

What in holy hell had come over him?

That kiss had blown his mind so completely, he'd forgotten about his dad. The long years that Mom had mourned him. The pain and stress of his dad's disgrace, which had brought on Mom's premature death from heart failure.

Wes had been furiously angry about that. For years.

Now look at him. A brief kiss from a beautiful woman could make him forget everything. His sacred mission, *poof*, gone. Thinking with the little head.

God help him. Like he needed another thing to feel guilty and conflicted about.

Four

They signed documents as Fake Elvis belted out the second ballad she'd chosen at random to a distorted karaoke track. The man had a beautiful singing voice, deep and rich and resonant. She couldn't make out why she felt like this. Perched on the edge of a cliff so high, she couldn't see the ground.

The song was so overused, it had become meaningless. Or so she'd thought. With Wes next to her instead of Jareth, her perception shifted, and she heard it as if for the first time. The simplistic lyrics now seemed not trite, but poignant. The song sounded like a plea, a promise. It was full of hope, like a tiny candle flame in an immense darkness.

And it was making her cry. Damn. She couldn't get sappy, not with a guy she didn't know, who might be completely unbalanced. A guy who was doing her a dangerously lopsided favor, which put her at a huge disadvantage. For nothing more than the entertainment value, and the vague hope of getting laid.

Ironic that she'd chosen this song, about tenderness and love and fidelity. She'd been so cut off from her own feelings. Tenderness was the key. It always had been. It was her missing piece. Her secret wound.

She'd gotten many things in life, wonderful things, to be grateful for. Wealth and privilege and opportunity, even a certain measure of fame and celebrity. But no tenderness. Not from her dad—that was certain. And she'd freely chosen Jareth, who wasn't tender either. After a while, he hadn't even pretended to be.

Why would she do that to herself? No wonder that song had always seemed silly to her.

Then Wes Brody appeared on the scene, teasing and clowning, paying her lavish compliments, kissing her hand, garlanding her with flowers, draping her in lace. Offering to help solve her complicated problems. Asking nothing in return but the pleasure of her company. Some men were just like that. They flirted, in the same unconscious, habitual way that they breathed.

Still, that kiss had shaken her, soul deep.

The last chord of the karaoke track faded away. The colorful disco lights ceased to spin. Ronnie tucked the bouquet into the crook of her elbow and clapped vigorously.

"Thank you," she told the singer. "That was beautiful. I'll never forget it."

Fake Elvis looked gratified. "My pleasure, Mrs. Brody."

Yikes. Mrs. Brody? That felt strange.

Outside the chapel, she looked up at the sky, breathing

deep as the constricting, oppressive fear finally lifted. She'd done it. At what cost, she didn't know yet. But whatever the cost, she wouldn't force her cousins to pay it. Thank God…and Wes Brody.

Her phone buzzed, and she pulled it out. Speak of the devil. Twelve unanswered messages. Eight unanswered calls. Aunt Elaine, Caleb, Marcus, Maddie, Caleb's wife Tilda, biting their nails, as well they might be, with Moss-Tech hanging in the balance.

"Are they checking up on your marital status?" Wes asked.

She nodded and opened the group chat, entering, Safely married. Breathe easy.

She showed it to Wes. "Short, sweet and nonspecific," she said. "I'll tell them about you later. I don't feel like dealing with histrionics right now."

"One thing at a time," he said.

"Myra and Sam and Joseph all threatened to call my family, but I told them I'd fire them," she admitted. "Not that I actually would, but I put on a good show. They're furious with me. But I'm used to fury. I grew up in a house steeped in fury. I barely notice it."

"You don't deserve that," he said.

"How do you know that?" she asked, with a teasing smile. "I could be completely wicked. You don't know."

"Oh, but I do," he said. "You're as good as gold. I'm sure of it."

Her face went pink. "That's very sweet. And so was all of this." She lifted the veil, the bouquet. "White lace and flowers and rings. And just marrying me to begin with. You saved me from disaster and disgrace and life-long guilt."

"It was an honor and a privilege."

He sounded like he meant it. There she went again, all sentimental because of a few offhand, gallant remarks that cost him nothing.

Jareth had never pretended that marrying her was an honor or a privilege. He'd been too busy reminding her of what an honor and privilege it was to be chosen by him. What a lout. And this was the first time she'd finally seen it clearly. What in the hell had she been thinking?

Ronnie lifted the veil off her head, trying not to damage the flowers, and folded it over her arm. "Well. Guess I'd better go back to the hotel and get myself a new room. It's late. Shall we meet tomorrow morning for breakfast?"

"But you should celebrate," Wes said. "You pulled it off. Against all odds."

"No, you pulled it off," Ronnie said. "You saved my bacon."

"But you had the nerve to seize the opportunity," he insisted. "That was brave."

"You put such an attractive spin on everything," Ronnie said. "My lawyer saw it in a very different light. The poor guy almost had a stroke."

"How's this for an attractive spin? Come up to my room for dinner. No expectations on my part. Call your people, tell them where you'll be and the room number. Have them check in on you periodically. All I want is to wine you, dine you and make you laugh."

She giggled. "You're overdoing it, Wes."

"We should mark the occasion. We'll call the front desk and book you a new room. They can run a fresh key up to you while you're relaxing over your appetizers and wine."

Oh, hell with it. Agreeing to dinner seemed the least

she could do, considering the hellfire and brimstone that he'd saved her from. "Just a glass of champagne," she hedged.

"Whatever. We've got a lot to talk about, now that we're husband and wife."

As if it were choreographed, his limo pulled up. She slid into the cushy leather seat. Wes joined her and took her hand. "I bet you haven't had anything to eat since before the speech."

"Actually, not since dinner last night," she admitted. "I'm always too wound up before a speaking gig. Just coffee. And those drinks we had at the bar."

He looked scandalized. "Good God, Ronnie. I'm surprised you're on your feet at all. Let me feed you."

"I am a bit hungry, now that I think about it."

The ride was short. On their way through the hotel lobby, Ronnie was grateful not to encounter anyone she knew. Her ugly interchange with Jareth had been horribly public. Word had certainly gotten around. People would draw their own conclusions as to why a recently dumped woman would return with a fresh man in tow, and none of those conclusions would flatter her.

But to hell with them all. She was a married woman. And even if she weren't, anyone who wanted to judge could sit on it and spin.

Wes pressed the button for the penthouse suites. The elevator had mirrored walls, showing every angle of her ravaged face. She dug into her bag for some makeup wipes and cleaned off the worst of the mascara smudges before the door slid open.

He used his key card to open his door, and beckoned her in.

Ronnie stopped short, and gasped.

The main room was lit up with what had to be a hundred candles. It was the only light in the room, other than the blaze of city lights in the picture window that opened onto the terrace. A lavish feast was set out on the table. Wine, champagne on ice, platters of tempting starters, silver lids covering up the entrées, fruit, salads.

There was even a wedding cake. It was miniature, three tiered, with a tiny bride and groom perched on the top. An enormous flower arrangement was the backdrop for the cake. The pale carpet was thickly strewed with white, pink and red rose petals.

"Wes," she whispered weakly.

"Kenji outdid himself," he said. "Do you like it?"

"Of course I do. It's romantic. Magical. It's just that… well, what part of 'business marriage' did you not understand, Wes? Did I give you the wrong idea?"

"How many times does a person get married in their lifetime? The occasion should be marked. A fuss should be made. I just married my celebrity science crush. That's worth a few rose petals. Shall we break out some champagne? I texted them to deliver dinner as we got into the limo, so the food should still be hot."

Ronnie was dazzled by the look in his eyes. Not just lust. She got plenty of that. Wes's gaze looked deeper, and some part of her couldn't help but hungrily look back.

Watch yourself, girl. Don't throw yourself over that cliff. You don't know him.

"Um…Wes?" she murmured. "You're not going to make me say it again, right?"

"I'll be the soul of propriety. Just let me pay tribute to your splendor. I see you, and my instinct is to fall to my knees and give thanks to a benevolent universe."

She laughed at him. "You are so full of crap."

"You betcha," he agreed cheerfully. "Blarney, my mom called it. The goal was to make her smile, at any cost. It wasn't always easy. I had to work like a bastard sometimes to make it happen."

Ronnie hesitated. "She had...troubles?"

"After my dad died, yeah. There was a long stretch with no laughing. But I kept at it. I made it my business to make her smile. I had it down to an art."

"What a good son," she murmured.

He popped the cork on the champagne bottle and poured. He passed her a glass with a flourish. "Can I take your jacket? I'll get you a plate of starters."

She hesitated before she let the jacket slip off her shoulders. Beneath it, she wore a low-cut ivory silk camisole with delicate lace insets. The room was warm, but she felt so bare, so vulnerable. She instinctively shrugged her hair forward, like a shawl.

The appetizers were delicious. Seared langoustines, morel mushrooms, foie gras croutons, delicately pan-fried crab cakes with mango-papaya salsa. Every bite tasted divine. The champagne was delicious and fizzy and cold.

But what she really wanted was more about him. He was a tantalizing mystery.

She licked the fruity salsa off her fingers and studied his face. "How old were you when your dad died?" she asked. "If you don't mind me asking."

"Almost ten," he said.

She winced. "I'm sorry you lost him so soon. Same with me and my mom."

"How old were you when it happened?"

"I was seven," she said.

He nodded. "That's very young to be motherless."

She nodded. "I had to fight for my memories. My father was furious after she died. He thought she'd betrayed him in some way, so he didn't want to remember her, or to let me remember her. He burned all the pictures of her, and all her personal things."

His eyes widened. "Good God, Ronnie."

"But Aunt Elaine and Uncle Bertram had some pictures, and some home movies they'd filmed that featured her and me, as a baby and a toddler. They made a video for me. So that I would at least know what her voice sounded like."

"I love them for doing that," he said.

She savored a wild mushroom. "Me, too. Do you remember your father well?"

"Not as well as I would like. Certain things. He was a tough guy. Kind, but stern. We butted heads. I got into trouble as a kid. I broke windows, got into fights, went places I was told not to go. We got into it. After he died, I felt guilty for a long time for being such a naughty little jerk. I wished I'd been a better boy for him."

"He wouldn't have wanted you to feel guilty. If he was kind, like you say."

"I like to think so. I know how hard it is to keep a memory vivid. Now it feels like one of those stars in the sky that you can only see when you're not staring straight at it. I'll get a random flash. The way the light hits a room, a familiar smell, a man wearing a hat like Dad wore, and for a second, I've got him. Then poof... gone again."

"Yes," she said. "Yes, that's how it is for me, too."

He served her the next course, as tempting as the last. Warm artichoke panache, poached green asparagus with balsamic vinaigrette, baked lobster and squash manicotti. Every bite superb. Her appetite had awakened. No sound but the clink of forks.

"I had no idea how hungry I was," she said.

"I'm glad you're enjoying it," he said, refilling her glass. "I chose the hotel for the chef. Hedonist that I am."

"You do treat yourself well," she said. "How did you get started at being a venture capitalist?"

"My dad's life insurance was the seed money," he said. "It was a generous payout. Mom managed it well. It covered my education, and there was some left over, so I played with it." He gave her a crooked smile. "And for the most part, I won."

"Lucky you," she commented.

"I guess." He looked at the locket at her throat. "Is the locket a sentimental piece?"

She touched the trinket that always hung at her throat. "Yes," she admitted. "And if it looks like something a seven-year-old might wear, that's because it is. My mother gave it to me before she left for Sri Lanka. That last trip." She snapped open the latch and showed the photo of Naomi Moss that her mother had cut to size and tucked inside it. "So that I could look at her anytime I wanted and remember how much she loved me, until she came home. But she never made it back."

He looked away for a moment. "Damn, Ronnie," he said.

"Sorry," she murmured. "You asked."

He wiped his eyes. "I did," he agreed, leaning closer. "May I?"

She nodded, and he lifted it up to look at the photo. "She looks exactly like you."

"So they tell me," she said. "I can't see it. But I suspect that's why my father has so much trouble with me. He looks at me and sees her."

Wes snapped the locket shut and rested it against her throat. "That's unfair."

"Maybe so, but I have now exceeded my quota of bitching about people who have done me wrong," she said. "They will not define my life. I'll be fine, even without *The Secret Life of Cells*."

"Without it?" He sounded alarmed. "What do you mean, without it? They're not canceling the show, are they? Why would they do that?"

"Jareth was one of my producers. He's the Fadden in Fadden Boyle Productions. He canceled it to punish me."

"What an asshole! He'll regret that."

"I hope so," she said. "I had ideas and scripts ready for another three seasons' worth of shows. Who knows, maybe I can eventually take it to another production company. I need to meet with my entertainment lawyers, and pore over my contract."

"Go to all lengths necessary," he said. "I don't know how you do it, but you make cell biology sexy."

"Thank you," she said. "I loved doing it. It seemed like I could do more good by fostering science literacy in kids than I could working in MossTech's research and development department. I loved that feeling. Like I had a real mission."

"You have to continue," he said. "The world needs it. And I'll make it my personal business to see that you do."

Heat rushed into her face. "Gee, thanks," she said demurely. "One thing at a time, though."

He nodded and stroked the wedding ring on her hand with his fingertip. "It looks nice on you," he said.

"Yours, too." She smiled at him. "It's certainly more

comfortable than Jareth's engagement ring. I'm so grateful that I don't have to wear the damn thing anymore. I
have to get it back to him, ASAP."

"You didn't like that ring?" He sounded surprised. "It
was such a big, impressive rock."

"Sure it was, but the setting ruined all my favorite clothes," she said. "And it never felt at home on my
hand."

"Out of curiosity, if you were to pick the perfect ring,
what would it be?"

"Pearls," she said promptly. "I love pearls. They're
alive. But Jareth hated that idea. He said, 'Pearls just
don't pack a punch.' Now that I think of it, that's why I
prefer them. They don't glitter. They glow, like the moon.
They're formed inside a living organism. I'm a biologist,
so I love it that a sea animal created something so perfect inside its own body. It makes me feel connected to
the sea, and the animal world."

"Pearls," he murmured. "Duly noted."

She was alarmed. "I wasn't hinting that you get me a
ring! Don't even think about it. I'm already far too much
in your debt and I have no way to repay you."

"Don't worry about it," he soothed. "It's a random
question. A get-to-know-you game. Like that stuff you
do on social media when you're procrastinating. Take
this quiz to see what jungle animal are you, what flavor of potato chip, which kind of cheese, which Beatle,
which Hogwarts House. That kind of thing. I'm just es-
tablishing your baseline."

"Ah." She settled into her chair again, cautiously mol-
lified. "Okay."

Wes refilled her champagne glass. "A toast," he said.

"To last-minute fixes. To eleventh-hour solutions. To un-expected saves."

She raised her own glass. "To new friends."

"Hell, yeah." They clinked glasses. The sweet bell tone of the crystal glass was diamond sharp, like all her heightened perceptions.

Their eyes locked, and her face heated. "No giving me that look, Wes."

"Sorry," he said. "How about we distract ourselves? With wedding cake?"

She was grateful for the change of subject, and the wedding cake was a marvel of miniature artistry. Three tiers, the bottom around eight inches in diameter, then a five-inch, and on top, one the size of a cupcake. All three were clothed in chocolate fondant, dark, milk, white and ruby chocolate, marbled together. The miniature bride and groom on top, the size of plastic toy soldiers, held hands. Smiles were painted on their tiny faces.

"It's adorable," she said. "A shame to cut into."

"Inside is a dark moist chocolate cake of smoked Peruvian chocolate with a hint of rum. Sounded decadent and good. Just one more little detail, since it is now—" he glanced at his watch "—midnight plus three minutes." He opened a little box next to the cake, which was full of tall, thin white candles. "I asked for them to provide thirty," he said, inserting them into the perfectly marbled frosting until the small cake had a close-set crown of candles. "Tonight, it's all about candles."

Ronnie was moved. Jareth never thought to mark her birthday, and certainly her father hadn't, so it never occurred to her to celebrate it. "Wes, that's so sweet!"

"Oh, but it will be." He used the candle lighter the hotel had provided to light them. The flickering ring of delicate, ethereal candles looked beautiful, like flower stems.

He smiled at her over the flickering light. "Make a wish."

The wish made itself, but she pushed it away. It was childish, unrealistic. It should be enough to just enjoy a lovely evening with an attractive man who made her feel good. It would be silly to grab for more, even in the privacy of her mind. She had to let tonight be tonight, and just enjoy it. She blew the candles out.

Wes laid out two dessert plates that had been provided and passed her the knife. She took out the candles, and sliced two wedges from the bottom tier, offering one to Wes.

"Don't we have to do that ritual where we feed each other wedding cake? Isn't that a ceremonial necessity? About nourishing each other, and all that good stuff?"

She lifted an eyebrow. "We don't need to put on a show for anyone."

"So let's put on a show for ourselves. Don't we deserve to be entertained, too?"

Hah. She was more than entertained. Wes Brody was walking seduction. If she started hand-feeding him bites of dessert, she would be taking one more shuffling step toward the abyss. Or more like a giant, stumbling stride.

But she was in the game now. "Hold still," she said, scooping up a bite of cake. It was tender and goopy, and she had to get both cake and frosting on the end of the fork.

Wes accepted the bite. His eyes closed, and he let out a growl of pleasure. "Oh, wow," he murmured. "Sensual. Complex. Aromatic. Addictive."

Everything she could say in response felt suggestive and flirtatious.

Wes scooped up a forkful of cake and held it up for her.

It was a marvelous burst of flavors. The chocolate was deep and bold and smoky, the cake melting, tender and buttery, the frosting creamy, with delicate aromas of cinnamon and rum, and behind it, a faint hint of fiery pepper and sea salt.

But she kept her eyes shut. She couldn't look at him. It felt like total exposure. As if she were naked, letting him watch while she touched herself intimately.

Where did that erotic thought come from? That vivid thought was the final step. Over the cliff she went. She wasn't going to deny herself this experience.

She opened her eyes and stared at the naked desire in his face. Unafraid of it, because it mirrored her own.

It was a moment outside of time, outside of the rules and expectations that had governed her life; the *should*s and the *can't*s and the *absolutely not*s. They melted away into nothing as shimmering awareness filled the air. It stole through her, lighting her up. Making her feel weightless, buoyant, larger-than-life.

The movement was imperceptible, but suddenly they were closer to each other. So close, the slightest movement would make them touch.

She liked this distance. The glint of beard stubble, the faint bump on his nose, the sweeping line of the hairs of his straight eyebrows. The sexy points of his square jaw. His lips were full, well shaped, sensual. His lashes were thick, on heavy-lidded dark eyes.

She couldn't resist any longer. She leaned forward,

pressing a swift, exploratory kiss against his lips, and rocked back, shocked at herself.

Just a brief contact, but her lips felt a hot, tingling glow, and a sweet ache for more.

Wes looked startled. "Ronnie," he said. "This isn't what you said before."

"I changed my mind," she said.

They gazed at each other for a breathless moment, and then he slowly reached out to her face. He cupped her cheek, slid his hand into her hair, making a sound low in his throat, an incoherent groan as he pulled her close and kissed her.

It started out tentative, and then bloomed into something hotter, sweeter, wetter. Hunger surged. It made her want to whimper and cling, to plead for more of him.

Wes let go, unsteady. His face was flushed. "Whoa," he said. "We have now reached the far end my self-control, so you should get in touch with the front desk. Get yourself a room. We'll talk tomorrow, in the café, over coffee. Where it's safe."

"Not necessary," she said.

His eyes narrowed. "Meaning?"

She felt brazen, reckless. She'd blasted past all her limits. She was out in no-man's-land. Free to be anything, do anything, all night long. "I'm not going anywhere."

"Help me out here, Ronnie," he said.

"You said it yourself," she said. "How many wedding nights does a person have in one's life? The occasion should be marked, right? A fuss should be made."

He cleared his throat. "But this is the direct opposite of what you said before. So I just need to be sure that you—"

"I'm sure," she said.

"I feel like I've always known you," he said. "It's like I've been waiting for you. I know it sounds corny, like a cheesy pickup line, but I swear, it's true. No blarney, no bullshit. I have never felt anything like this."

"I feel it, too," she said simply.

"But that doesn't mean we have to race forward top speed," he said. "We can take it slow. You can't walk this back, once we do the deed. It could be like a massive landslide. We could wake up and find ourselves in a different life. All the rules changed."

She placed her hand over his. "I like the way that life looks."

"You won't feel like I pressured you, after? I don't want you to think that I—"

She put her finger on his lips. "Just kiss me."

Five

Wes was under her spell, commanded by some absolute authority deep inside him that could not be gainsaid. He'd once gotten caught in a riptide while surfing. This felt similar, but this time, he wasn't struggling to swim free, or fighting to stay above water. He was letting the wave pull him wherever it wanted him to go.

Take me. Own me.

The kiss was urgent, desperate. Like they were dying of thirst, and this was the first water they'd seen. Her lips were sweet and ardent. He stroked the perfect, elegant curve of her spine, the flare of her hip.

She pulled back, tugging the silk camisole out of her pants, and pulling it off over her head. She flung it away, and tossed her hair, her eyes dazed with arousal. Lips red from kissing, parted from panting. She kicked off her shoes. Her body was so perfect. Those high, plump breasts in the flesh-toned satin bra begged for his palms to caress them.

"You're so beautiful," he said. "I just can't help bleating that out over and over. It blows my circuits."

She looked him up and down, her gaze lingering on the erection straining against his pants. "The necessary circuits appear to be working just fine."

"Nope, no problem there. I don't have any diseases, by the way. I don't expect you to trust my word, but I could fish my last bloodwork results out of my email, if you want, and show you the—"

"I trust your word," she said.

Her words reverberated inside him like a bell. He was moved by her trust, but the more she trusted him, the worse it would be when his hidden agenda came to light.

Tell her. Just tell her now. Everything.

It trembled on the tip of his tongue. But as he opened his mouth to blurt it all out, Ronnie laughed. "Good heavens, Wes. You look like you're afraid of me. I don't bite."

"You're perfect," he said softly.

She let out a snort. "You'll know the real me soon enough." She seized his tie. "Until then, bask in my fictitious, fleeting perfection. I'll enjoy it while I can."

There were so many ways he could reply to that. He wanted to tell her that she could be perfect without having to be perfect, but that sounded ridiculous. She unhooked the front of her white trousers and let them drop to the floor.

She unfastened the front clasp of her bra and lifted it off. Sweet holy God. Her breasts were rosy and high and pointed, little hot pink nipples, taut and hard. She hooked her fingers into the side of her boy shorts and tugged them over her hips. She had a sweet, ginger-toned swatch of ringlets over her mound.

There she was, in just a wedding ring, and her mother's locket.

Her eyes were full of amusement as she waited. "Well, Wes," she said. "As opening gambits go, I don't know what more to do to convince you that I'm up for this. Short of tying you to the bed."

He cleared his throat as he wrenched his tie loose. "That won't be necessary."

"I also have a clean bill of health and thank you for bringing it up. Before I came to Vegas, I thought it right to check my health status before I got married. Fresh starts, new beginnings, that kind of thing. I haven't been with Jareth since months before that, for various reasons. Also, I'm on the pill. So there's that."

"Wait," he said. "Months? How on earth?" His mind had seized upon the most incomprehensible bit of random information in that list.

"I haven't seen him in a while," she admitted. "We've both been extremely busy professionally."

"You were wasted on a self-satisfied clod like him," he said.

"Hmm. I can't say I disagree, but I'm afraid of what that says about my judgment."

"Nothing," he said. "The spell is broken. We hereby close the door on him. This is a private party, and he's not invited."

That earned him a smile. "Charming, as always," she said. "And yet, despite all your brave words, you're fully clothed. What gives, Weston Robert Brody?"

She shook her hair back. The locket gleamed, and the

candlelight painted the tender curves and hollows and swells of her body with a dim, gold-toned glow.

He jerked open the buttons of his shirt, his fingers clumsy with eagerness. "Just letting you take the lead," he offered.

"That's a lovely thought, but don't lag too far behind. I wouldn't want to lose you." She reached out and pulled the buckle of his belt loose. "Pick up the pace, mister. You have husbandly duties to perform."

Oh, sweet, sweet husbandly duties. He got the cuffs loose and unfastened his pants. Ronnie drifted around behind him like a graceful ghost, moving silently on bare feet, and lifted his shirt off his shoulders. She let out a sigh, her smooth fingers running over his shoulders, sending shivers over his skin. "You're beautiful," she whispered.

He shucked his pants and briefs as he turned to face her. Stark naked.

Ronnie's gaze slid along his body. Over his shoulders and chest, his belly, his groin. His aching erection, jutting hopefully in her direction.

"Well," she murmured. "You look ready for anything."

"I've been fielding this erection on and off since the moment you walked out on the stage this morning," he admitted.

Ronnie laughed softly. "Aw. How sweet."

"Not the adjective I'd choose, but whatever."

He took her hand, and lifted it to his lips, pressing a kiss against her knuckles. Then he pressed it against his chest. "You're safe with me," he told her. "Absolutely in control. This is all for you. All for your pleasure."

Her eyes dropped, the brilliant blue veiled with the long, sooty dark lashes. "All?" she said, her voice throaty, as her hands slid lower, and then lower still, into the tangle of dark hair between his legs, grasping the shaft of his penis and squeezing it tenderly. "There's…um…a lot of you."

"Not much I can do about that," he said, and then caught his breath, choking off a groan. He wanted her to feel powerful, pampered, adored. "But I'll make it work for you."

Wes kissed her hungrily, stopping from time to time to gasp for air at the wild sensations that jolted through his body with each slow, sensual caress. He could hardly believe she was real. So warm and smooth. Over her shoulder, he admired the stunning view reflected in the picture window. That hair swinging at the small of her back. The curves of her bottom. Perfect.

She let go of his penis to wrap her arms around his neck with a low, incoherent whimper of need. Wrapping her leg around his thighs. He followed her lead and lifted her up, holding her backside so that she straddled him.

Best feeling on earth, to have that deliciously scalding hot, secret, wet female flesh pressed against his aching rod. He held her right where she needed to be, so she could move, stroking the tender pleasure points up and down his shaft. A tantalizing taste of the deeper contact that would follow. She arched, in trusting abandon, reaching with one hand to grip him. Holding him more firmly against herself as she pulsed her hips against him. "Can I?" she asked, breathlessly. "Do you mind if I—"

"Please," he choked out. "Best thing in the world. It's killing me, but don't stop."

She laughed under her breath, through the panting eagerness as she voluptuously pleasured herself against him. Head flung back, eyes shut, her lower lip caught between her teeth. Her panting turned to whimpers as the tension built…and built…

And broke, explosively. She arched and he caught her, holding her tight as she abandoned herself to pleasure. Sobbing at the wild intensity of it.

He watched her come with fascination. It was long and delicious, and it finally faded to a subtle, rippling throb. Her body was limp and soft, trusting.

The intimacy made him feel awestruck, humbled. And so aroused he could barely breathe.

"My God," she whispered. "My God, Wes. What the hell was that?"

He nuzzled her neck, licking away the sweat. "I'd call that a promising beginning."

Finally, she lifted her head, and stroked his flexed biceps with a low murmur of approval. "Aren't you getting tired of holding me up like this?"

"I could hold you up forever," he said. "But I'd like to use my hands to touch some other parts of you. Not that holding your ass isn't absolutely the high point of my entire life. It's silky and round. Perfect as a peach. But there are other places I want to explore."

"Do you have any particular destinations in mind?" she murmured teasingly.

That smile on her face made him euphoric. "I intend to leave no part untouched."

"Well," she said, "in that case, put me down."

He set her onto her feet, and sank to his knees, nuzzling her belly. It felt right, to be in this position, unthreatening, paying tribute to her beauty, passionately appreciative. As a bonus, he got a good, close look at her beautiful smooth thighs and that swatch of hair. Her sweet, hot scent. Intoxicating.

She looped her arms around his neck as he embraced her hips, pressing her closer. His face to her belly. He put his hand on the inside of her knee and stroked slowly upward, glancing up. "May I?" he asked.

She gave him a jerky nod. Her hands shook as his fingers brushed her slick, hot core. He caressed the whole length of the seam of her labia, up…and down. Slowly, tenderly massaging that taut little bud of nerves hidden in her secret flesh.

He slid his fingers inside her clinging wet warmth, swirling and flicking with his thumb. Swirl…and flick. "I want to lick you," he said. "You're the most beautiful thing I've ever seen. Is that all right with you?"

"Do you want to go to the bed?" she asked. "My knees are like jelly. I don't think I can stay on my feet."

He swept her into his arms, which made her laugh. Every giggle felt like a win. So did every orgasm. He'd just keep racking up points, as long as he could. Until he…well.

For as long as he could. He'd just leave it at that. He shoved the painful and unwanted thought away and slammed the door on it.

The king-size bed in the next room was heaped with rose petals, the bed turned down. A long-stemmed red rose lay on the pillow. Nice touch. Kenji knew his stuff.

He set her on the sheet and shoved the puffy comforter to the side, sending petals scattering in every direction. He stroked her hair, draping it over the pillow. Her eyes were shadowy pools of mystery. Her locket gleamed in the dim light.

Their eyes locked. They were completely in tune. If it weren't for his secret agenda, this would be perfect. A peak life moment to burn into his memory forever.

Her brows drew together. "What is it?" she asked. "Is something wrong?"

Damn, now she could read his mind, too. "No," he lied. "Nothing's ever been so right. I just feel…unworthy." True enough. All things considered.

But Ronnie shook her head, smiling. "You're wonderful," she said softly.

He hid his face against her throat. The locket felt hot and smooth against his lips. Her skin was so cloud soft. He kept his eyes shut as he made his way hungrily along her sweet body with his lips, taking his time, exploring every curve, every hollow. He lingered for a long time at her breasts, licking and sucking them delicately as he stroked between her thighs. Seeking out the spots that made her sob with pleasure.

She came apart around his hand, clutching his fingers. Best sensation on earth.

Well, almost the best, but only one thing could top it. And he was getting there. Taking his own sweet time, doing it right, making her come, making it count. Over and over. That was the way. Keep the bad thoughts away. Allow nothing but pleasure.

She was so limp and relaxed after that last orgasm, she barely noticed him parting her legs, folding them high and wide so he could admire every detail of that perfect flowerlike female beauty. He settled between her thighs and put his mouth to her sweet, tender bits, worshipping them. Lapping up her magic balm. His senses overwhelmed. Systems on override. He couldn't think about inner conflict. He couldn't think at all.

That was the trick. Just spend all his time like this. In heaven.

Time slipped loose of its moorings and they drifted in

a dreamlike state. Intoxicated with her flavor and scent, her texture, the sounds of her low voice vibrating through her body as he pleased her. Her silky texture. The tiny shivers of delight that vibrated through her.

The energy was slowly building to another climax. He settled in to make it an explosive one. Building her up, then easing her back, again and again. Letting her hover near the brink, over and over, until finally she'd had enough torment.

She grabbed his hair, silently demanding that he finish, so he did, with passionate enthusiasm. Fireworks, delicious and pulsing, right against his mouth.

She cried out, shivering with her helpless response.

He cuddled up afterward, gathering her limp body into the shelter of his arms, pulling the comforter over her. His body throbbed with urgency, but he was goddamn well waiting until it was the right time, the right move. With this woman, he would take nothing for granted. He would treat her like blown glass.

He buried his nose in her fragrant hair and inhaled her sweet scent until her pulse slowed, and her breathing calmed. Finally, she shifted, snuggling against him.

"And?" Her voice was dry and husky from the panting. "What about you?"

"What about me? I'm in heaven. You're spectacular. I love making you come. It makes me feel like a total sex god. I love it. I could specialize in this. Sign me up."

She chuckled as she slid her hand over his belly and then tangled her fingers in his pubic hair. She stroked his stiff, aching penis.

"And what shall we do about this?"

He dropped a kiss on her forehead. "Whatever you feel like doing," he said lightly. "Your call. Do what you want with it. Or not. You could sleep now and I'd still be happy. Or you could use me like your own personal sex toy." He rolled over, putting his hands behind his head. "Like I said. I'm at your service."

She tilted her head thoughtfully. "Are you playing games with me? What is that?"

"I'll tell you what this is," he said. "One, it's me keeping my ass covered. Two, it's the fulfillment of my wildest dreams. You, climbing aboard me, pleasuring yourself with my body…yeah. If that's a game, then yes, let's play games. I just intend for you to win every last one of them."

She tossed the comforter off, and climbed on top of him, throwing her leg over him. "I will take you up on your generous offer to be my sex toy."

Wes looked up at Ronnie, swaying over him, backlit by the candlelight, and the spangled city lights outside. Her hair brushed and tickled his belly, his chest.

He struggled to keep his voice from shaking. "I'm all yours," he said.

Six

Ronnie stared at him, stretched out beneath her. He clasped her waist with his huge, strong, but exquisitely gentle hands, waiting for her cue.

She felt so odd. As light as air. Lit up and floating, like a lantern. Every bit of her glowed with a hot, total awareness, as if every cell of her body was sexually aroused, from her toenails to the tips of her hair.

And it felt so good.

So different from her other experiences. Not that there were many. She'd concluded long ago that she must be one of those people for whom sex wasn't a top priority. Which, oddly enough, was one reason she'd originally thought that a match with Jareth might actually work. Because it had soon become evident to her that it wasn't much of a priority for him, either. He was a busy man, lots on his mind. So she thought, okay. They'd be a cerebral couple. A marriage of the minds.

She felt anything but cerebral with Wes. She felt hot, carnal. And she loved it.

Wes cupped her breasts tenderly. "You're so gorgeous."

"You're pretty fine yourself," she told him, touching that stiff, thick phallus lying against his taut belly.

Wow, that was a lot of aroused man, but she wasn't intimidated by his size. She relished it. He made her feel hungry. Greedy.

Wes gripped himself at the base, holding his shaft up. "Like this?"

"Perfect," she said, poised over him, sliding her hand over the smooth, hot surface of his glans, making him shudder and groan. "It's okay?"

"Heaven," he ground out. "Everything you do. Perfect."

Well, great. So she could do no wrong. She swayed over him, undulating as she captured him. Petting herself with him…and then slowly…slowly…sinking down… and taking him deep inside.

The two of them made the same sharp, panting sound, between a sob and a moan.

She braced herself against his chest, unable to move, but Wes instinctively shifted, making it all perfect, effortless, delicious for her. He gripped her waist, angling himself, and they settled into a slow, pumping rhythm. Gliding, slick, fabulous.

She melted around him. His thick shaft caressed her inside, a slow, sensual lick, caressingly stroking over and over her unexpected new sweet spots. Maddening, tantalizing, sweet. It drove her wild.

Her nails dug into his chest. She incited him with whispered gasps to pick up the pace. He gripped her hands, deepening his strokes as they both sought that tantalizing promise of bliss, like a shining trail that glowed in her head, brighter and brighter, terrifying, inevitable.

It crashed through her. She was lost to the world. Pure delight blazed through her, body and soul.

After, her face was pressed against his damp chest. It rose and fell, but she still heard his heart, thumping madly against her cheek.

She lifted her face, gazing into his dark eyes. He looked somber. No dimples, no joking around.

"And…how are you?" she asked.

"Flattened," he said. "It's never been like that for me. I mean, I love sex. Always have. Tons of fun. What's not to love? But I never, you know. Felt myself dissolve into stardust or anything like that. I think I passed out. That was wild. Deep."

"Me, too," she admitted. "Is that a good thing? For you? The stardust, and all?"

His lips twitched, and his penis, still inside her, stiffened afresh. "I'm great."

"I love it," she told him.

His arms tightened around her. "Thank God," he said. "The stakes felt so high."

She felt moved, realizing that he felt insecure, too. He seemed so confident.

She shifted on top of him. "Do you want to go for round two?"

"I'm always ready, but I don't want to get greedy," he said. "Let's not overdo it."

"And leave me high and dry?" she teased, her body

clenching jealously around him. "Though I'm anything but dry." She slid off him, lying on her side, her thigh flung over his, and tugged at him. "You on top this time," she told him.

"You sure?" he asked.

"I crave it," she said. "I love how hard and solid and hot you are. I want to hold you with my arms and legs. Give in to my voracious desires, Wes. Don't make me wait."

He rolled obligingly on top of her, still mostly inside, and reorganized their bodies. Him on his knees, her arched back, legs folded wide. Stroking her clitoris cleverly with his thumb as he thrust inside her.

She shivered and sighed, abandoning herself to pure sensation. Bracing her feet against his chest as he skillfully teased her into another orgasm.

After that, he kissed her slowly and sensually as he pulsed slowly inside her.

"You okay if I finish now?" he asked.

That was a question she'd never even known a man could ask. Wes had a level of skill, self-awareness and self-control that she'd never encountered before.

"That's fine," she said. "I'm in a state of perfect grace. I just want to watch you come. The last time I was too overcome to even pay attention."

"You got it," he said. "Tell me if it's too much."

And they started up again, eyes locked. Bit by bit, the movements deepened. Urgent, slick, hot. Against all expectations, she felt that charge of pleasure start to build.

Wes sensed it, of course, and shifted, instinctively hitting just the angle that she needed to nudge her closer to the brink, stroking her while he stared into the depths of her soul. That marvelous, melting vortex was opening up for her, pulling her into a wild, chaotic storm of passion.

Sometime later, she stirred against him. They were a damp tangle of limbs. She dropped a kiss on his big shoulder. "Um…" she murmured. "I think a shower is in order."

"Can I join you?"

She started smiling at him and realized she couldn't stop. "Sure."

The shower in his suite was huge, faced with black marble, with multiple showerheads at every angle. She tried twisting her hair up into a knot as she sudsed up under the jets of water, but it came from every direction, plus she was wildly distracted by the glorious spectacle of Wes Brody, naked and wet. All that lovely width and breadth and bulk of him, all that cut, defined muscle. To say nothing of his magnificent érection.

He followed her gaze. "Down, boy. Think of it as a tribute to your female power. It doesn't matter how tired I am. One glance at you, and whammo, I'm ready."

"Do you want to—"

"No, no. We'll take a rest. There's more where that came from, and there'll be more tomorrow, too. And the day after that. Here, let me rinse you."

His clever hands, slick with foamy soap, caressed her expertly under the pounding water. Before she knew it, she was squirming around his hand, her hair clinging to her shoulders, soaked in the spray as she worked herself into a deliciously melting climax.

She was floating, weak in the knees, clinging to his shoulders as Wes rinsed off the soap. He toweled her off, still dripping, dragging the fluffy towel carefully all over every inch of her skin before he dried himself off.

"Sorry," he said into her ears. "That was a crime of opportunity. You felt so good. Hot and pink and perfect. All that slippery soap. Too much for me."

"I forgive you," she told him.

"Hey, it just occurred to me that there's a whole lot of tasty food on the buffet table, and the champagne's still in the ice bucket. The food's cold, but I don't care."

That idea sounded excellent, to the point of daring to put weight on her wobbly knees. They swathed themselves in the terrycloth robes the hotel had provided and made their way through drifts of rose petals and scattered clothing to the living area.

The food was even better the second time around. The icy cold champagne tasted like the elixir of the gods. Artichoke tarts, peppers rolled around creamy cheese, red olive paste spread on crusty bread, the tray of cheeses, the leftover manicotti…delicious. Her usually spotty appetite felt like a blast furnace. Between the two of them, they polished off most of the food, and nibbled on another piece of cake. So good.

Afterward, Ronnie opened the door to the veranda, and strolled out to lean on the railing, looking at the wild, clashing colors of Las Vegas.

Wes followed her and leaned on the railing beside her. She glanced around, taking note of the architectural design that protected them from the view of anyone else on the top floor of the hotel. Luckily. Considering what she had in mind.

"So," he said, in a neutral, careful voice. "Do you feel as if the occasion of your wedding night has been marked appropriately? Has an adequate fuss been made?"

She gave him a teasing smile. "What do you think?"

"Not what I asked," he countered. "I'm sticking with my original question."

"Are you feeling insecure, Wes?"

He shrugged. "Maybe. I'm human, and this is important. Tell me how you feel."

She leaned against his shoulders. "I have never felt like this in my life," she told him. "I didn't know sex could be this good. But this is the thing."

"What's the thing?" he demanded.

"You've awakened some part of me that's sexually insatiable," she informed him. "Now, you have to deal with it. You'll have your work cut out for you, satisfying my voracious appetites."

He looked delighted. "How voracious are we talking? Just to get an idea."

"Ravenous," she said emphatically. "A panther on the prowl."

"Awesome," he said, as she jerked the sash of his robe loose. It fell open, and she closed her hand around him, enjoying the throb of his heartbeat against her palm.

"I know you think it's more gentlemanly to let me rest," she said. "But I don't want you to be a gentleman right now."

"I'll be however you want me to be."

She shrugged off her own robe. She felt so hot, the chilly breeze against her damp hair was intensely stimulating. She turned her back to him. Bending at the waist, arching her spine. Parting her legs. "So?" she prompted. "Fulfill me."

"You got it," he rasped, reaching for her.

Seven

Something tickled Wes's nose as he floated up to full consciousness. Light, against his eyelids. With every breath, he felt a faint tickle.

He opened his eyes and saw rose petals fluttering as he exhaled.

He was alone in the bed.

He sat up quickly, looking around in irrational panic. Ronnie wasn't in the bedroom. He didn't hear movement in the front room. He didn't hear water running in the shower. Just silence. Shit. She'd panicked. Bolted.

The intense depth of his disappointment startled him.

He slid out of bed, hesitating for just a moment before heading into the main room.

That night had been astonishing. White-hot. But he'd known she might panic and withdraw from that intensity. It was a classic move.

They barely knew each other, after all, and last night had laid them bare. He'd felt more known and seen by her than he'd ever felt. Dangerous secrets notwithstanding.

He kicked away bruised rose petals as he strode through the room. The candles had burned down over the course of the night. It was late morning. Evidence of their late-night feast was everywhere. His clothes were still scattered around the floor, but Ronnie's shoes, pants, jacket, purse, all gone. His heart sank lower.

The towering flower arrangement and rose petals seemed to taunt him. She'd left the bridal bouquet behind, still in the vase that Kenji had selected for it, as well as the box that held her folded flower wreath and veil.

Evidently, she didn't plan to conserve it as a keepsake. That hurt.

The bathroom door flew open. He spun around with a gasp.

Ronnie stood in the bathroom door, looking dewy and fresh, dressed in yesterday's white suit. Her hair was brushed out, loose and wavy and gleaming.

She looked bright-eyed and rosy, considering how little sleep she'd gotten.

"Good morning," she said. "You look startled. Were you expecting someone else?"

"I just thought…" His voice trailed off.

"Thought what?"

He shrugged self-consciously. "You were nowhere to be found, and I didn't see your clothes or purse, so I thought…"

"That I panicked? After the most fabulous night of my whole life? Hah. You'd need a crowbar to pry me away." She held up her purse. "I took my purse into the bathroom because it had my makeup wipes and brush and mascara and emergency lipstick. And I had to rescue my clothes from the floor and recycle them."

"We could order you some clothes," he suggested. "If you want fresh stuff. There's a boutique in the hotel. More than one, I think."

"What I want is to retrieve my suitcase from Jareth's room. But I don't want to engage with him right now." She took her smartphone out of her purse and scrolled on the screen. "Yep, eight calls from him last night. Texts, too."

"What does he want?"

"To know where the hell I am, and when I'm coming back," she said.

"A) none of his goddamn business, and B) not in this lifetime," he said.

"Exactly. But I will try to be classy, if I can," she said.

"I bet you he's not in the room," Wes said. "He's out prowling the hotel, hoping to run into you. He's realized that he miscalculated, so he's too agitated to sit in his room. He's been awake all night, worrying about it. Now he's trying to track down his errant heiress. He wants to herd her into the barn, where he thinks she belongs."

She winced. "Ouch. I suspect that's a pretty accurate assessment of his attitude."

"Let's go now," he suggested. "I'll knock, and if he answers, I'll say I'm delivering the travel crib that he requested for his baby. If he doesn't answer, just go in and grab your stuff. I'll stand guard outside to make sure he doesn't surprise you."

She looked troubled. "Why do I feel like I'm stealing?"

"Because from his point of view, you are," he said.

"You're taking back something that actually belongs to you. Something he thought he owned. Your life, your choices, your freedom. He's liable to be ugly about it. By the way, who booked the room?"

"Me. It was my idea, and therefore, my expense. Jareth isn't much for treating."

He grunted in disapproval. "All the more reason to check him out of the room. Freeloading asshat." He pulled on some jeans. "I'll get dressed, and we'll get your stuff."

He tossed on a sweatshirt, shoved his feet into some shoes, and they were on their way. In the elevator, he took her hand. It was cold and clammy as they went up to the penthouse floor. He hated it that she felt nervous about running into that worthless tool. He wished he could take Jareth aside for a talk before she saw him. Give him a remedial lesson in manners. A pointed lesson.

She stopped by one of the doors in the hallway and pulled out the key card.

Wes knocked, waited a few moments, knocked again. Nothing. "You're clear."

Ronnie lifted her key card. The door flashed green. She went in and got to work, scooping stuff out of the closet and cramming it into a hanging bag and a large suitcase. She disappeared into a bathroom and came out with a beauty case and a bouquet of brushes and combs.

Then, the electronics. She coiled the cables, gathered up chargers, packed up her laptop and tablet and stowed them all in a large leather computer bag.

"All done?" he asked, his eyes fixed on the elevator.

"Almost," she said. "I just need to leave…this."

She took her wallet from her purse and extracted the

diamond ring from the pocket where she had stowed it the night before. She tucked it into a black velvet ring box.

"I feel as if I should leave a note with it," she said. "But anything I could write to him would either be scolding or insincere. Neither is particularly classy."

"Silence is fine," Wes said, loading up with her suitcase and garment bag. "He'll hate that. Silence gets my vote."

Her mouth twitched. "Agreed." She set the box on the bed. "All done."

They returned to his room with the bags. "It's official now," he said. "That chapter of your life is over. Congratulations."

"Thanks." She sank onto the couch, staring into space. "I am so glad that I didn't marry him. Why couldn't I see it? It would have been a miserable, suffocating disaster, and it would have ended in a horrible divorce. It's so clear to me now."

"I'm glad that you were spared all that," he said. "We should celebrate."

But Ronnie didn't look quite ready for celebration yet. "It's a good thing that I forced Jareth into a corner," she mused. "It's the only way I would have seen who he really was in time to bail."

"You would have figured it out," he said.

"But at what cost? I can't believe how blind I was."

The troubled look in her eyes was making him nervous. "Are you okay with how all this went?" he asked. "It's a lot. All these massive changes, and then me, all up in your face, demanding your attention."

"I'm fine with the changes," she said. "I'm just...not sure what happens now. My whole life, I've had a clear path in front of me. First it was getting good grades in school, then doing well at university, then at grad school, and then getting the fellowships, the grants, etc. Then the research and development job at MossTech. Then it was the show, which absolutely consumed me for the last few years. I haven't stopped to breathe since it all began. I had a mission, and suddenly it's gone. There's no path anymore, and it feels…strange."

"You'll find a new path," Wes said. "You're not the type who can stay pathless for long. And your mission hasn't changed. The mission chooses your path for you."

"You're probably right, but I still feel lost."

"I have a suggestion," he said. "It might seem suspiciously self-interested but hear me out. The perfect time for soul-searching is when you're pathless. It gives you an ironclad excuse to do things you otherwise would never let yourself do. Fun, frivolous things. Run away with me. I stole that guy's bride, and his wedding, so why not go three for three, and steal his honeymoon, too?" He paused, studying her face. "You were going on a honeymoon, weren't you?"

"No," she admitted. "Jareth had to be in LA by tomorrow, for some meeting or other. There was just no time for it."

"I see," he murmured. "Well, lucky me. I have the time for a honeymoon."

"Really?" she said. "Aren't you a hotshot venture capitalist with your fingers in scores of pies? I would have expected a guy like you to be constantly on the go."

"Oh, I hustle plenty," he assured her. "But I had already planned some downtime for myself, as it happens. I had some business meetings to take care of here in Vegas earlier this week, then I hung around to see your keynote address. After that, I was going to do something fun.

Maybe climbing in the Rockies, maybe go to Amalfi, to get the renovations for the villa started. Or Greece. I love Greece. I have a yacht docked in Argostoli. I could take you sailing. We'll hug the coast of Kefalonia, sleep on the boat, stop at all the hidden coves and beaches, skinny-dip in bright blue water, eat fried fish and moussaka and red olives and tzatziki and gyro flatbread, and wash it all down with cold, crisp Robola white. My local favorite. You'll love it."

She looked impressed. "Sounds wonderful. You go all-out, don't you?"

"Why hold back? Life is short. But take your time. What are your dream destinations? Anything your heart desires. What setting would make Veronica Moss relax enough to start dreaming up what's next on her path? That's the question. And whether the answer is snorkeling in the Great Barrier Reef, or climbing Machu Picchu, or floating under the Bridge of Sighs in a gondola in Venice, or trekking in Nepal, I am up for it."

She looked intrigued. She had no clue how passionately willing he was to follow through on this. Showing Veronica Moss a good time sounded like the most fun he'd ever had in his life. He'd go to any lengths to persuade her.

"Sounds decadent," she murmured.

"Oh, it is," he told her. "Your people warned you that I was a hedonist, right?"

"They did," she said. "And you proved it last night. Beyond a doubt."

"I could prove it again right now," he offered. "I could keep proving it all day. Or all week. Indefinitely. I am so inspired."

"Sounds like great fun," she said. "But first, coffee."

He brewed her a fresh pot while she called the front desk and checked out of the room that she'd shared with Jareth. After that, she accepted the cup of French roast, and gave him a thoughtful, assessing look. "You've finished your business in Vegas?"

"That is correct."

"So have I. Vegas has served its purpose for me. I'm no gambler."

"You gambled on me," he pointed out.

"Good point," she murmured. "Time to cash in my winnings, then."

That look of sensual speculation in her eyes made hunger surge inside him. "I like the sound of that," he said. "Say the word."

"Come with me to Seattle. If you want to," Ronnie offered. "I'm not quite ready to leave the country with you yet, but I'd enjoy the process of being persuaded. In the meantime, we can have some honeymoon fun in the Pacific Northwest. It's as beautiful as any other vacation destination. Let me check some flight times."

"Don't worry about flight times," he told her. "I'll fly you to Seattle."

"Fly me?" she said, startled. "You have your own plane? Here?"

"My pilot is standing by. Tell me where you want to go, and I'll take you there."

"Impressive," she murmured. "Okay. First stop, Seattle."

"That's where your family is based?"

"Yes. I've been back and forth to LA for the last few years, and I rented a nice apartment there, but I kept my condo in Seattle, even though Jareth tried to persuade me to sell it. I like having my own space when I'm in town. All of us Mosses were born and bred in Seattle. MossTech is there, so my dad lives there, my aunt, and my cousins. Though technically they're my first cousins once removed. My father was ten years younger than my uncle Bertram, and my mother was fifteen years younger than my dad, which makes for some confusing generational mixing. But all my cousins are older than me, Maddie by a couple of months. They feel more like siblings. We're very close. They're wonderful people. You'll like them."

"Will I meet them when we get to Seattle?" He held his breath for her reply.

"Maybe Maddie and her husband, Jack," she mused. "The boys are both traveling right now. Everyone is extremely busy, but Jack and Maddie are more available than the others, mostly since they can't seem to stop honeymooning. They're both between jobs, too, so they're taking their time and living it up."

"Sounds like fun," he remarked. "We should try it."

That earned him a luminous smile. "Right now they're spending a lot of time up in Cleland, this gorgeous little town in the Olympic rainforest. Jack just bought a beautiful house in the forest that I love. Minimalist cubes of glass, in the woods, in a cathedral of mossy trees, right on a river canyon with waterfalls. And when they're not there, they're at the beach house my aunt Elaine gave them as a wedding present."

"Living the dream," he said approvingly. "What about your male cousins?"

"They're in Southeast Asia right now. Tilda and her little girl, Annika, had to go to a friend's wedding in Jakarta, so Caleb decided to go along. Marcus is on one of his trips to Indonesia, and his brand-new wife, Eve, is off at some genetics think tank with her team, working on taking Corzo, her grain project, to the next level. And my dad's in London, thank God. Everyone is scattered to the four winds. The only family member that I'm sure that I can introduce you to is my aunt Elaine."

Wes felt a rush of guilty relief. Maybe he wouldn't get busted right away.

"Let's get moving," he said. "I'll pack up. We'll grab a bite and get on our way."

"Sounds good," she said. "I've worked up quite an appetite, hanging around with you. I'll just get some fresh clothes and change while you pack."

Wes stared around the jumbled bedroom, the wildly disarranged bed, his scattered clothes, drifted rose petals, burned-out candles, and started throwing stuff into his bag, more haphazardly than usual. He felt too excited and jittery to be methodical.

Under the circumstances, he shouldn't feel this excited, but Ronnie exerted a huge gravitation pull on his mind, dragging him into the present moment. Away from anger and pain. The fear of what would happen in the future.

But it was all still there, lying in wait.

After that horrible incident with Tilda and Caleb last year, his window of opportunity would be brief. Once Caleb heard his name, it was all over. He'd have only hours in Seattle to search for whatever documents Naomi Moss might have shipped home from Sri Lanka in that container twenty-three years ago. The truth was in those files, if they still existed.

One thing was certain: if this gambit didn't work, he'd have to apologize to the souls of his dead parents, pray that they forgave him and suck it up. Accept that he would live the rest of his life not knowing. And then get the hell on with it.

Last year, he'd been in a different headspace about it. Much more angry and punitive. The Mosses had been trying to do a hostile takeover of Tilda's father's company, so he'd given Tilda Riley a copy of his father's file so she could attack the Mosses with it.

That had been an unqualified disaster. Far from ruining the Moss family, Tilda had joined forces with them. She'd fallen in love with Caleb Moss. She'd married the guy, for God's sake.

Tilda had never used the file because she hadn't believed what was in it, and she hadn't wanted to destroy the family she'd just married into or betray the man she'd bonded with. So she'd sat on it. And when Wes showed up to do the job himself, she stole his original documents and burned them. To protect the Mosses.

Which left him with no hard proof. Nothing but the copy of his dad's journal, which he'd transcribed himself. There had been a sheaf of lab notes that went along with his dad's journal, but all of them were gone. Incinerated in Caleb Moss's fireplace.

The disaster had culminated in Wes getting attacked by Caleb Moss in a hotel room. Caleb had concluded that Wes was having an affair with Tilda. So Wes opened the door, fresh out of the shower, and found himself in a no-holds-barred fistfight. Not his finest moment. It was safe to say that Caleb would remember his name.

But if Tilda and Caleb hadn't mentioned him yet, he might have a window of opportunity before the Moss family sent him straight to hell.

Not that it would matter. When Ronnie found out, he'd be in hell already.

Eight

"You're attracting a lot of attention," Wes said. "Is this normal for you?"

Ronnie glanced around and saw six pairs of eyes snap away. "Pretty much," she said. "Maybe they recognize me from the keynote address or the conference program."

"I thought of the hotel restaurant because it's excellent and conveniently close. I forgot about you being a celebrity. I should have taken you someplace more secluded."

"No." Ronnie squared her shoulders, meeting the gaze of anyone who had the nerve to stare at her full on. "Let them stare. I'm finished with being self-conscious. Last night just burned it all out of me, and it feels great to be free of it."

Wes made an approving sound. "You can hardly

blame them for looking. You're on fire. I couldn't look away if I tried."

Good, because that was exactly how she felt. She was glad that it showed. "Don't try," she said, throatily. "I like when you look at me." She took a fat, ripe strawberry, and scooped up a generous, quivering glop of Chantilly cream with it, then ate it slowly and sensually, in unhurried bites, licking away creamy goop, and then licking each of her fingers in turn. "I can't get over it. Everything tastes so good today."

She caught her breath at the fierce blaze of hunger in his eyes.

"You are merciless," he said softly.

"It's all your fault. Yesterday, I was a harassed, mealy-mouthed people pleaser, scurrying around and trying to keep the world from getting mad at her. Today, I'm a naughty, hedonistic, selfish bad girl, intent on my own pleasure." She stroked his finger with her own, a long, slow caress. "And I'm going to let you help me. Because you're oh…so…good at it."

He cleared his throat. "Ronnie. Not fair. We already checked out of the room."

"There will be other rooms," she said. "And it'll keep."

"That's for sure," he said fervently. "The question is whether I survive the wait."

They finished their coffee and headed through the lobby toward the exit as Wes checked his phone. "The limo is waiting, bags stowed. We can head to the airport."

"Ronnie!" A sharp, angry voice called from behind them. Jareth's voice.

This was going to be interesting. But she didn't feel

that sinking dread she had expected, buoyed up by Wes's warmth. Like he said, she was on fire.

Ronnie turned, bracing herself. Better sooner than later.

Jareth strode toward her, eyes darting suspiciously between her and Wes.

"Where in the hell have you been, Ronnie? You had me worried sick! You didn't answer your phone, you didn't answer my texts, you weren't in the room—"

"I didn't want to talk to you," Ronnie said. "I still don't."

"That's too bad, because we still need to talk about our future," Jareth lectured. "Being part of a couple is all about compromise, finding a solution that works for both people, and you just don't seem to get that. I regret upsetting you yesterday, but you drove me into a corner, Ron. You left me no choice."

"There's always a choice," Wes commented.

Jareth fixed Wes with a gaze. "Excuse me? Did it look like I was addressing you?"

Wes smiled and shrugged.

Jareth snorted and turned to her. "Get it through your head. Going forward, I won't indulge your irrational impulses. Especially not when they affect our future."

"We have a problem, then, Jareth," Ronnie said. "Because irrational impulses are kind of my thing right now."

Wes gave her a grin, which Jareth caught. He turned to Wes. "Whoever you are, this is a private conversation," he said sharply. "Buzz off."

"No, actually. I'll stay right where I am." Wes's tone was implacable.

"What…?" Jareth glared at Ronnie. "Do you know this person, Ron?"

"I do now," Ronnie replied. "Jareth, this is Wes Brody. My husband."

"Husband?" Jareth's face darkened. "If this is a joke, it's in extremely bad taste."

"My bad taste is no longer your problem," Ronnie said. "I will never embarrass you again, Jareth."

"But I…" Jareth's mouth worked. His eyes moved frantically between her and Wes. "You couldn't have. You didn't actually…"

"Marry him? Yes. I already had the chapel booked, after all. I used the same time slot that I booked for you and me. We just got a new license at the courthouse."

"But who *is* this person?" His voice got louder.

"A new friend," Wes said. "Ready to help out in a tough spot. Your loss is absolutely my gain."

Jareth's mouth twisted, and for the first time, she realized his uncanny resemblance to her father. God, she'd come so close to yoking herself to this. Falling right back into the miserable trap of her childhood. The nearness of her escape made her dizzy.

"You slept with him?" Jareth's voice cracked with outrage. "You married the very first man you saw, and then just…just took him to bed? That's disgusting, Ron!"

"Watch your mouth," Wes said evenly. "If you want to keep your teeth in it."

Jareth shook his head. "A complete stranger? You have multiple degrees, Ron. I know you're not a stupid woman. But this is idiocy! He'll take you for every penny he can get, and it will serve you right!"

"I had to keep my promise to Aunt Elaine," she said. "You let me down, so I had to improvise. I'm lucky to have found a solution, thanks to Wes."

"You won't be thanking him for long," Jareth said.

"And when this bites you in the ass, I will be watching the floor show and slow-clapping, Ron. Because he's got an agenda, too. Everyone does. Always. You're too goddamn innocent to grasp that."

Wes took her arm. "This sounds like our cue. Let this clown eat our dust."

"Yes," Ronnie murmured. "I can't say I'm enjoying this."

"I'll make it my business to inform everyone in the business how crazy you are!" Jareth shouted after her. "No one will work with you! You're finished in television!"

Ronnie stopped and turned, drawing up to her full height. "Are you threatening me, Jareth?" she asked. "Is it time to get MossTech's legal department involved?"

"If you do, play them a video of this conversation," Wes said. "As soon as I saw his face, I hit the record function." Wes held up his phone and touched Play.

Jareth appeared on the screen, shot from below, at Wes's waist level. His flushed face looked grotesque from the strange angle as he harangued her.

"...in the hell have you been, Ronnie? You had me worried sick! You didn't answer your phone, you didn't answer my texts..."

Wes stopped the video. "I've got every word that comes out of your mouth. All the way to the end, where you threaten her with career-ending slander." He tapped at his phone. "Saved to the cloud. Ass officially covered. So, you were saying?" Wes gave Jareth a thin smile. "Or are you rethinking it?"

Jareth's mouth worked. He looked at her. "I thought you were better than this," he said.

"I thought you were, too," Ronnie replied.

She let Wes take her arm and lead her away, mortified by the tears blurring her vision. He drew her through
the big revolving doors at the front entrance of the hotel.
Dammit, why? Jareth wasn't worth her tears.

Wes opened the door of the limo that idled at the curb,
and helped her in, then slid in beside her, his leg pressed
against hers. He wound his fingers through hers. "I'm
sorry you had to go through that," he said. "I should've
taken you out a side door."

She laughed. "And sneak away like a fugitive? I have
nothing to be ashamed of. And it's not your job to protect me."

"Actually, it is," he said thoughtfully. "Protecting each
other falls under the umbrella of the spirit of marriage
vows. And you're well worth protecting."

Ronnie squeezed his hand. "Aww, a lovely thought,
Wes, but getting embroiled with Jareth Fadden was my
poor judgment, not yours. That unpleasant conversation
had to happen. I'm glad it's over."

"Well, for the record, you were amazing," he said.
"Indomitable."

She looked at him and snorted. "Sweet talker."

"No way," he insisted. "You were calm, elegant, polite. You never lost your cool. Your voice was smooth
and golden. You were in complete control of yourself.
Whereas he degenerated and had to be put sternly in his
place. Which you did, like a goddess."

"Quick thinking, to record him with your phone,"
she told him.

"As soon as I saw his face, I knew it would get ugly,"
he said. "A record of his bad behavior will keep him
honest. Force is the only language a troll like that un-
derstands."

Ronnie shook her head. "I don't know how I got my-self into that." Her voice still uneven. "He was nicer early on, but after a while... God. I don't know. I guess I was just so used to Dad being cold and belittling. I didn't no-tice anything out of the ordinary when Jareth was, too. It just seemed, you know. Familiar. I knew I could survive it because I always have. And he seemed to value me. For things that I could do, the way I looked, my ability, my credentials." She paused. "And MossTech," she con-cluded. "Mostly MossTech."

"Bastard," Wes muttered.

"Thanks for standing by me," she said. "It would've been harder alone. Particularly if I were still unmarried."

"I'm honored to help."

The warm, tender look in his eyes made emotion swell inside her, and when her phone rang, she was so flus-tered, she hit Talk before she saw her cousin Maddie's name on the display. Whoopsy-daisy. Another intense conversation, hard on the heels of the last.

"Maddie?" she said.

"Ronnie! Do you know how many times I've tried to call you? Where are you?"

"I'm on my way to Seattle," Ronnie said. "And you're a fine one to complain. You've let me stew in my own juices for weeks at a time without answering my calls or texts when you get into one of your moods. Remember when you ran off to Hawaii?"

"This is different," Maddie said. "Since you insisted on inserting yourself into Gran's marriage mandate, that means you have to endure our scrutiny."

"Fine," Ronnie said. "Scrutinize to your heart's con-tent."

"So you're married? That's what you said last night in the group chat."

"Sure am," she replied, leaving it at that.

"So how is it that when I called Jareth to congratulate him, he told me that you guys had a huge fight, and that you stormed off, and that you weren't married at all?"

"Maddie, what on earth possessed you to call him?"

"Why not? I figured, the guy's like my brother-in-law now, and I have to make an effort, right? I was trying to be nice. I am so confused right now."

"You haven't said anything to Aunt Elaine, or Caleb, or Marcus yet, have you?"

"Um…not yet," Maddie said. "Not that it matters, babe. If you're not married by now, you've missed the deadline, and that's that. Happy birthday, by the way."

"Thanks," she said.

"Look, Ron. I get it, if you choked at marrying Jareth," Maddie said. "I just regret that you wrote yourself into the mandate to begin with. Bad time to criticize, but that move was as dumb as a box of rocks. But there's just no point in lying to us about it."

"Listen up," Ronnie said. "Short version—I am married. Legally married, shortly before midnight yesterday. I'm just not married to Jareth."

Maddie was quiet for so long, Ronnie started wondering if the connection had broken. "Maddie? Are you still there?"

"Wait. Hold on. So you're married to…who?" Maddie's voice was small.

"His name is Wes. I met him yesterday. He offered to help me out. A last-minute save, to keep MossTech out of my dad's clutches. So I took him up on it."

"And this was after you stormed away from Jareth?"

"To be precise, he stormed away from me," Ronnie said. "He refused to go through with the wedding. He wanted Dad to get MossTech and take it public. He was thinking of the eventual payday. I was on my own. Then I met Wes."

"Ron." Maddie sounded subdued. "That's so risky. You know that we care much more about you than about MossTech. I hope you haven't gotten yourself in trouble."

"Not at all," Ronnie assured her. "The situation is under control. He's coming back to Seattle with me now."

"He is? That's interesting." Maddie harrumphed. "Hmm. So Jareth turned out to be venal, calculating and self-serving, eh? Goodness me, Ron. I'm shocked. Shocked, I say."

"Don't start," Ronnie begged. "I'm already so embarrassed, okay?"

"I'm not scolding you," Maddie soothed. "It's just a relief that now I can freely tell you what a condescending butthead he is."

"Um…yes," Ronnie agreed. "He tried to coerce me by putting *The Secret Life of Cells* on the line. I wouldn't back down, and he canceled it to punish me."

Maddie gasped. "That bastard! Your beautiful show! Annika will be crushed."

"Yes, but I'm glad it's over. He would have destroyed me, by inches."

"Well, none of us ever liked him. We all hoped that you'd come to your senses in time, so we were appalled when you put yourself into the mandate."

"It was stupid, yes," Ronnie admitted. "But you know what? I think that things are looking up. I think my luck might be changing."

"Oh, really?" Maddie's voice changed. "Do tell! Is it the new guy?"

Her eyes flicked up to Wes, who was looking away from her, trying not to smile.

"Can't really talk right now," she said. "Please don't say anything to Aunt Elaine or Caleb or Marcus yet, okay? Give me a minute. Let me breathe."

"On one condition," Maddie said. "Dinner, tonight. I want to meet him."

"Maddie, it's a little early to start inflicting my relatives on—"

"The hell it is! You're married to the guy! Meet us for dinner, or I call Gran right now. What do I call him?"

"I called him Mr. Mysterious when I first saw him," Ronnie said.

Wes's smile stretched into a grin. "Cool," he said.

"Aren't you guys still up in Cleland?" Ronnie asked.

"No, we're at my place in the city. Jack had meetings, and I had a client consult. Let's go to that place down the street from you. Café Kuna. Can you get there by eight?"

"I think we can manage that."

"Great. I'll book a table. Can't wait to dissect your new husband. I just hope he's worthy of you, and that you have an ironclad prenup. You do have a prenup, right?"

"Yes, yes, I have a prenup," she soothed. "Signed, witnessed, notarized, filmed for posterity, and already in the possession of my lawyers. Have no fear. My ass is covered. And I really dodged a bullet, Maddie. I feel...I feel like I'm floating on air."

"Is that so?" Maddie sounded like she was smiling. "I like the sound of that. I haven't heard you sound that way since we were kids. I look forward to meeting the guy who can make Veronica Moss bubble and froth and float on air."

"I do not bubble or froth!" Ronnie protested.

"We'll see for ourselves tonight. Till then!"

Ronnie let the phone drop. "My cousin Maddie and her husband are meeting us for dinner tonight. Hope that's okay. They intend to grill you left, right and sideways."

He grunted. "Fun times."

"Actually, it will be," Ronnie said. "Even if you're being grilled, Maddie is always fun. She's like a sister to me, and Jack's a great guy. You'll like them."

"I'm looking forward to it. Will I meet your dad, too?"

"No, he's in London, and will be for a while yet, if the Fates are kind. I stay as far from him as I can. I got my own place as soon as I could. A condo on the waterfront. I never could get comfortable in Southern California. I'm an Emerald City girl."

When they boarded, Ronnie was impressed with the luxurious interior of his Fabiolet Eagle.

"I love to fly planes," Wes confided, as they strapped themselves in. "But when I'm in business mode, I get someone else to fly me."

"Very nice," Ronnie said. "So it's true. You deny yourself nothing."

"Nope. I know it's extravagant, but I invested in the company, Fabiolet Eagle. Cutting edge eco design. As of the time I bought it a couple years ago, it had the most efficient thrust-to-weight ratio of any plane on the market. It uses sixty percent less fuel, emits fifty percent less carbon. It's a great little plane."

"My cousins Caleb and Marcus would love it," Ronnie said. "I can't wait to introduce you."

Wes picked up the bucket of ice on the shelf and set up two champagne glasses. "I'm looking forward to it," he said. "I've heard tales about them."

"Yes, they do tend to make the news," she agreed.

"You must have the celebrity gene in your family," he said. "Along with the good looks. I've seen pictures of them. But you look completely different. Just as good-looking, but no family resemblance at all that I can see."

"They say that I look like my mom," Ronnie said. "Any luck that I had on that score can be attributed to her."

He popped the cork of the champagne. "And your dad?"

"I've seen pictures of him when he was young," Ronnie said. "I suppose he was a good-looking man. But his face is so pinched and severe now, you can't see it anymore."

"Last night, when I was helping drape your veil, it occurred to me that it should've been your mom to do that," Wes said. "But maybe she was there. Watching over you."

That gave her a sharp pang of longing. "I like to think so," Ronnie said.

"So, you said that your dad burned all her stuff, right?" Wes touched her locket. "This is all you have left?"

"I have a few things that Aunt Elaine salvaged for me," she said. "Some photographs, some fine jewelry, a couple of scarves, a few of her favorite books. Old, dog-eared paperbacks. And those home videos that I told you about."

"Did they ship her things home from Sri Lanka after she died?"

"They must have," she said. "I was only seven, so I didn't have much of a grip on the details. But I'm sure that Dad threw out everything she'd ever touched." She paused. "But now that I think about it, my aunt must've dug that stuff up from somewhere."

"You should ask her," Wes said, pouring out the champagne. "A couple years ago, I was selling property that had belonged to my dad. I found a box of old files, and it had a journal in it. Dad's last journal. It was amazing, the way it made me feel. Like he was right there with me. I could hear his voice in my head. So if there's anything to be discovered, I recommend making the effort. As part of the new project. Veronica Moss, seeking her path into the future."

"That must have been an incredible feeling. What did the journal say?"

"It wasn't so much the content, which was mostly about his job. It was his distinctive way of talking. Now and then, he mentioned me and my mom." He lifted her hand and kissed it. "Ask your aunt if there's anything to look through. You might find something meaningful. It's worth a shot."

"It's a good idea," she told him with a smile. "I will."

Wes lifted his champagne flute just as sunshine slanted through the window, illuminating the sparkling wine into a brilliant, crystalline glitter. "To reconciling the future with the past," he said.

"Amen," she said.

She glanced out as the plane banked and turned, looking at the blue sky and the pale brown desert scrub below, now giving way to dry mountains. She felt so light.

Life was so shockingly different from yesterday. She'd been preparing to marry Jareth Fadden and braced for a long week of meetings with the production team to plan Season Four of *The Secret Life of Cells*. She was used to eighteen-hour days, sleepless nights, constant multi-tasking. She had a killer work ethic, like all the Mosses.

All that was gone, and she was sipping champagne, soaring over the desert in the private plane of the most attractive man she'd ever met, after a night of delirious pleasure. On the brink of a wild adventure. It felt great. She'd never been the type to put pleasure or excitement at the top of her list of priorities, but then, she'd never spent a day and night with a man like Wes Brody either. Call her frivolous, but this uncharted path into the future was a hell of a lot more fun than anything that had ever come before.

She finished her champagne and shook her head when he moved to refill her glass.

"Do we have privacy in here?" she asked.

"If I latch the cabin door," he said. "Do you have something in mind?"

"How long until we land?"

"Maybe another forty minutes before we start the descent," Wes said.

Ronnie set aside her champagne glass. "That's long enough," she said, unfastening her seat belt. A few steps took her to the cabin door, which she swiftly closed and latched.

"Ronnie," he said, looking intrigued. "What's up?"

"You, Wes," she said, in a low, husky voice. "Very soon."

His eyes widened as she sank to her knees in front of him, gripping his thighs. "Last night, you rocked my world," she said. She reached out, and tugged his belt, pulling the buckle loose. "Today, I feel like returning the favor."

He sucked in air as she unbuttoned his jeans and reached inside to stroke the stiff, thick shaft trapped in his briefs. Stroking it. Squeezing it. Freeing it.

She took her time. Slow, twisting strokes that made him arch and gasp, shuddering with sensation. His response made her feel powerful. Intensely aroused.

She took him in her mouth, savoring the groan of helpless delight that vibrated through his body. She wanted to melt him down. Drive him wild with pleasure. Exactly what he deserved, after what he'd done to her last night.

Luckily for him, she was a firm believer in balancing the scales.

Nine

Wes admired Ronnie's waterfront condo while she got ready for dinner. It was a beautiful space, comfortably decorated, overlooking the busy waterfront. It was open plan, with an airy living space dominated by huge picture windows that looked out at the water and a beautiful terrace with a view of the water. There was a comfortable grouping of rust-colored, crimson and slate blue couches and chairs and beautiful Persian rugs scattered over the gleaming plank flooring.

Twilight had given way to evening. Ronnie was freshening up while he paced, nervous as hell for this dinner date with the cousin.

He distracted himself by looking at her pictures and knickknacks, but he was too anxious to focus. This might be the moment of truth. Ronnie hadn't said his last name to her cousin, but she would when she introduced him.

Everything hung upon whether Caleb and Tilda had told the rest of the Mosses about his dad's file and journal.

And the fistfight with Caleb in the hotel room, of course.

Tilda might have kept it quiet. That incident didn't reflect well on her, though he understood her motives. Sneaking, stealing, corporate espionage, destroying evidence—it wasn't the kind of behavior a person wanted to advertise. And Caleb wouldn't be quick to admit where he'd gotten the black eye and the split lip. He'd probably told everyone that he fell off his bike. Macho idiots did stupid stuff like that. He knew that for a fact, being a macho idiot himself. But at least he was self-aware about it.

Of course, once Caleb and Tilda got back to town, the jig would be up. His best-case scenario was to get a handful of days to find out what he could about Naomi Moss's papers. Anything she might've sent home from Sri Lanka.

But the more time that he spent with Ronnie Moss, the less important the past seemed. He was using the most desirable, intriguing woman that he ever met in a way that was manipulative and dishonest. Mom and Dad would not have approved. If their positions were reversed, he would feel furious, humiliated. But what could he do? The damage was done. There was no going back. They'd made love. His fate was sealed.

He'd put himself squarely into the lying-scheming-bastard category.

Even if he came clean, and confessed everything to her right now, she would feel betrayed. He would lose her anyway. Along with his last shot at the truth.

He might as well hold out a little longer. Salvage something from this.

It was a long shot in any case. Jerome had burned Naomi's things. Ronnie didn't live in her family home, or even go there often. It was a lost cause.

And yet, here he was.

He wandered around looking at what she'd hung on her walls. There were a lot of candid shots of Ronnie's cousins. Then he came upon a column of three similar framed photographs of three extremely good-looking couples. Her cousins, paired up with their respective mates. Formal photographs.

That was Caleb with the blonde, ethereal Tilda, that one was Marcus, and there was Maddie. Three entirely different, distinctive types of extreme good looks. Maddie's husband, Jack, was Hollywood handsome in his own right, and Eve, Marcus's wife, was a stunner. Those big, luminous gray eyes, that gorgeous smile.

All three couples looked happy. Too happy to be stiff and self-conscious while getting their pictures taken. Laughing. Trusting their partners. Excited for the future.

Ronnie was the kind of woman Mom would've liked. That made it worse. His parents would've wanted him to be happy. They would have wanted him to take an opportunity like this and treat it with the reverence that it deserved.

He pushed the thought away, moving on to a photograph of Ronnie's parents. That was Naomi Moss, on the deck of a large sailboat, dressed in cutoff shorts and a bikini top, her red hair flying in the wind. A man was next to her. Dark haired, barefoot, in rolled-up linen boat pants and a loose shirt. He was laughing.

Jerome. Wes could barely see some subtle resemblances to Ronnie. The tilt of the eyebrow, the firm jaw. Ronnie was right; he'd been a good-looking man, in a sharp, chiseled sort of way. Ronnie wasn't in the photo. Maybe she wasn't born yet.

He moved on to the shelf over the fireplace, admiring the Emmy she'd gotten for Season Two of *The Secret Life of Cells*. He'd watched the awards ceremony on TV. There were shots of Ronnie, receiving the award, in a sequined black gown, her hair a mass of luxurious curls. And other pictures of her, receiving other awards: Excellence for Women in STEM, another for fostering scientific literacy in youth. She truly did have a mission, and she was fulfilling it with brilliance and generosity. She was a gifted, top-quality woman, and she deserved better than this duplicitous bullshit from him.

That reflection made him utterly miserable.

"Hey, there," Ronnie said, from behind him. "See anything interesting?"

He turned. She stood in the entryway to the corridor. "It's all interesting," he said, gesturing at the photos. "Look at you, rubbing elbows with the A-listers and stars. So you were in *Metabolize*? The Pixar film that won best animated film?"

She laughed. "Yeah, I voiced Molly the Mitochondria. That was fun. I met some movie stars. Going to those events is grueling, though. The expensive dress, the cameras, the scrutiny. It's stressful, but great publicity for the cause, so whatever."

"No, you crush it," he corrected. "These couples on the wall, are these your cousins and their spouses?"

"Yes." Ronnie's eyes softened. "Aunt Elaine insisted on formal photos for everyone, and they turned out well. They all look so happy."

He pointed at the sailboat photo. "And these are your parents?"

She moved closer, bringing a fresh, springlike whiff of flowers with her. "Yes, that's Mom and Dad, on their honeymoon. She was already pregnant with me. I think that's the only picture I've ever seen of my father smiling."

"I'd be smiling, too, if I were him. She's gorgeous."

Ronnie's hand went instinctively to her throat, touching the locket. "She looks larger-than-life to me," she admitted.

"Like you," he said. "And speaking of which, you look great. As usual."

She dimpled at him, smoothing her hands over her dress. "Flatterer."

It wasn't flattery, just a statement of truth. Ronnie wore a clinging gray sweater dress that hugged every perfect curve and swell of her body, a black belt accentuating her narrow waist. She had on black knit stockings and short black boots, and her hair was twisted up into a glossy knot on top of her head. Her eyes looked shadowy and mysterious, and her lips were cherry red. She looked gorgeous, vivid. Happy.

He wished he could enjoy that. That this thing between them could have made them both happy. Wildest-dreams happy, if not for his secret agenda.

Ronnie's smile faded. "Are you okay? You look tense. Subdued. For you."

"Just nervous about the grilling, I guess."

"Are you kidding?" Ronnie rolled her eyes. "Rest easy. Aside from saving me from the consequences of my silly choices, you just saved MossTech's collective butt, and my cousins' careers. You saved Uncle Bertram's legacy, and you saved my aunt Elaine from her own folly. You're golden, Wes. They'll love you."

Hardly, when the truth came out. He plastered on a smile. "Shall we call a car?"

"No need. It's a five-to-ten-minute walk, depending on how high my heels are."

"And how high are your heels?"

She struck a pose and gracefully kicked up one foot, showing him the moderately high heel. "Six-point-five minutes, by my calculations," she said.

"Lead the way," he said.

After the blazing sun of Las Vegas, the damp wintry chill of Seattle made him turn up his collar as they walked toward the restaurant. But he was grateful for any distraction from that sucking hole of dread in his belly.

If Maddie and Jack recognized his name, his idyll with this woman would be over.

He wasn't ready. He never would be. But into the doghouse he would go, and there he would stay, for the rest of his natural life.

Café Kuna was a small and elegant place, with a mellow, hushed decor. They went inside, but before the host could even speak, they heard an excited voice ring out.

"Ronnie!" They turned to see a gorgeous woman hurrying toward them, smiling widely. A handsome man with blue eyes followed her. She had smooth, golden-brown skin, a halo of tight black bouncing ringlets. Big amber eyes, bright with curiosity, darted between them.

Maddie seized Ronnie in a tight embrace. "You old married lady, you," she said, her eyes flicking to Wes. "Introduce me to Mr. Mysterious."

"Maddie, this is Wes Brody, my new husband," Ronnie said. "Wes, my cousin Maddie Moss, and her husband, Jack Daly."

Wes watched Maddie's face carefully, but she made no reaction to his name. Neither had Jack. He shook hands with the others, his knees weak with relief.

The moment of truth would come. But not tonight.

Wes and Jack were talking about Jack's ocean-cleaning, plastic-eating enzyme formula, so Maddie leaned close to her. "Ron!" she murmured. "He's great. Handsome, energetic, funny. And he seems real. Like Jareth never did."

Ronnie winced. "Can we pretend that relationship never happened?"

"Oh, don't be touchy. Jareth led you into Wes's arms, so he was good for that much. So what's up with the two of you?" Maddie lifted a well-shaped dark eyebrow. "Are you guys actually involved?"

Ronnie's blush spoke for her. Maddie's smile widened to a grin.

"I'm having so much fun," Ronnie confided in a whisper. "He's wonderful, but I hardly know him. My first thought was only about covering MossTech's ass, but then I started to realize that he's special in his own right. I just hope I haven't overloaded this relationship. We should be getting drinks, flirting, playing it cool. But we're married, for God's sake."

"I don't think it's overloaded," Maddie said. "I have a good feeling."

"Let's not think about it too hard, Mads," Ronnie begged. "I don't want to scare it away. Don't ask me any tough questions about him yet, okay?"

"I understand how you feel, but you know what? That guy is crazy for you. I can tell. I never got that sense from He-Who-Must-Not-Be-Named. He thought he was God's gift. I won't last long without asking questions, Ron. It's my nature."

"Oh, speaking of questions," Ronnie said. "Remember that photo album Aunt Elaine gave me when I graduated, with the pictures of Mom and Dad? Do you know where those came from? Does Aunt Elaine have a stash of my mom's stuff?"

"Well, yes." Maddie looked puzzled. "She rented a storage unit for the stuff that was shipped from Sri Lanka after the bombing. Didn't you know about it?"

Ronnie's neck prickled. "A storage unit? With Mom's stuff?"

Wes looked over them. "Storage unit?"

"Yes, of Naomi's stuff," Maddie explained. "She sent a container on a boat from Sri Lanka before she was killed. Gran went out of her way to intercept it. She knew Jerome would've burned it, and she wanted to preserve whatever she could for you. She would have stored it at her own house, but she wanted to keep it safe from Jerome."

"Yes, he tried to destroy everything that belonged to her."

"There wasn't a lot in there, as I recall," Maddie said. "Gran took me there when you and I were seniors in high school. She wanted help looking through the boxes for photographs for a graduation present for you. There were lots of books, some furniture. Old file folders. Random stuff. Clothes and shoes. Dishes, fabric, ceramics. Things like that."

"But why didn't Aunt Elaine tell me?" Ronnie asked.

"I think she intended to." Maddie sounded bemused. "But after we graduated, you took off like a shot, and stayed gone for a long time. Then Grandpa Bertram died, and I think Gran forgot all about it. Why did you think of it now?"

Ronnie glanced at Wes, who took her hand. "Because of a conversation we had," she said. "About reconciling with the past."

Wes spoke up. "I lost my dad when I was just a couple of years older than Ronnie was when she lost her mom," he said. "A couple of years ago, I found some old journals of his. It meant a lot to me. Like he was reaching across time."

"What a lovely thought," Maddie said. "All I remember is that the storage place was somewhere in Greenwood. Gran should have the address, and the key."

"Okay. I'll ask her tomorrow."

Maddie's eyebrows climbed. "So you're going to introduce him to Gran?"

"Should I be afraid?" Wes asked.

"Not in the least," Maddie said. "You saved MossTech. And she disliked Jareth. You're a much better bargain."

Wes inclined his head. "I'm gratified that you think so."

"Why can't we talk to Caleb and Marcus? They'll be thrilled."

"Not yet," Ronnie said. "There's plenty of time to tell them later. Same with Dad. Someone's going to tell him about this, if they haven't already, but no need to rush it. He's going to be so angry."

"Angry?" Wes looked around. "Angry why?"

Ronnie, Jack and Maddie exchanged glances, and snickered.

"He's always angry," Maddie explained. "It's his default state. Keep that in mind when you meet him. That way you won't take it personally."

"Okay," Wes said. "Thanks for the tip."

At that moment, the waiter came to the table with a bucket of ice and a bottle of champagne sticking out. Maddie pulled out the bottle and filled three flutes with the sparkling wine. "And now, my dear cousin, and my new cousin-in-law, I must make an important announcement," Maddie said, beaming. "I've been bursting to tell you."

"Oh, God. Are you pregnant?" Ronnie exclaimed.

"Twelve weeks," Maddie said. "We were waiting to be sure, but everything looks good. We don't know if it's a girl or a boy yet."

Many tearful hugs and much excited babbling ensued. It made her heart melt.

"I want to be there when you tell Aunt Elaine," she said. "I want to see her face."

"Soon," Maddie said. "After my next ultrasound. Not a word when you see her tomorrow. Tell me if you find anything interesting in the storage unit, okay?"

"As soon as possible," Ronnie assured her. "I'll call you."

"Let's go tomorrow," Wes said. "As soon as you get the address and key."

"You don't have to go with me," Ronnie said. "It'll be dusty and boring. Probably sad."

"All the more reason. You can't do a sad thing alone. Not on my watch."

There was a moment of startled silence. Maddie gave him an approving smile.

"Excellent," she said. "And for that show of touching

solidarity, you get a piece of the best chocolate-pecan pie you will ever taste."

In the midst of their laughter, Ronnie felt his hand under the table, squeezing hers.

It felt so good to have someone holding her hand, having her back. She'd tried not to need that with Jareth. To be self-reliant. Not jealous of what her cousins had found. The laughter, the tenderness, the trust, the ease. And now, a baby, too.

Suddenly, it seemed as if maybe she'd been blessed by that wild magic, too. It seemed greedy and dangerous to hope that it was real. Like asking for trouble.

But she couldn't seem to stop herself.

Ten

She was climbing a mountain. Crawling up bare, jagged rocks. Crawling through thorny plants. The wind was cold, and the sky was gray and threatening.

Suddenly, there was an opening in the rocks. She pulled herself up, and stepped through it, into a hanging valley. The grass a brilliant green. The clouds had broken into puffy white columns, with deep blue behind them. The ground was thick with flowers, and the fragrant breeze made the grass ripple, changing its nap like velvet when it was stroked. She gazed at the heart-stopping beauty in awe...

The squeak of the bedroom door made her eyes open. Wes poked his head in.

He smiled apologetically. "Didn't mean to wake you," he said. "I just wanted to check and see if you were awake and ready for breakfast. Go back to sleep."

She smiled, lazily. "I was having a really good dream."

He ventured inside, smiling. "Sorry I interrupted it."

She thought of the unbelievable pleasure that he'd showed her after they got back from Café Kuna as her eyes traveled over his magnificent body. "Reality is even better."

"Good to hear," he said. "Since you're awake, you should know that I went out and got breakfast from the coffee shop down the street. On the table is fresh orange juice, breakfast sandwiches, breakfast pastries and French roast with half-and-half."

Her belly rumbled, making them laugh, and Ronnie sat up, tossing her hair back. "That sounds delicious," she said, stretching, arms over her head. "I'm hungry."

He studied her naked chest with hot-eyed fascination. "Before I lose my head, the mission I set myself was to fuel you for the mission. Operation Reconcile with the Past."

Ronnie sauntered across the bedroom, taking her bathrobe from the hook. His eyes felt good on her body as she shrugged it on. She'd always felt self-conscious with Jareth when she was naked. Like he was judging, comparing, assessing her assets and her flaws.

Well, duh. Because he had been, constantly. Wes made her tingle and glow.

"First, coffee," she told him. "Must have coffee."

"On the double," he said.

Soon she was at the breakfast table, being freshly pampered. The sandwiches were delicious. Eggs with crispy bacon and melted Gruyère on crisply toasted English muffins. Gooey pecan-crusted cinnamon rolls. Lemon-blueberry scones. Tangy, fresh-squeezed orange juice. A big cup of strong, fragrant dark roast, with a shot of cream, just how she liked it. He'd noticed and remembered. How sweet.

He'd even gotten a bunch of sunflowers for the table. Flashy, cheerful, gorgeous.

It felt wonderful, having him in her own pretty space, sipping coffee. The sky was an ominous gray, and it was going to rain today, but she was inclined to see the beauty in any natural phenomenon that came along today. It was a survival skill that all Seattleites developed, with their constantly overcast skies and omnipresent drizzle.

After she finished licking the pecan goop off her fingers, she sighed with satisfaction. "I'm ready to face the past. I'll call Aunt Elaine."

Aunt Elaine picked up the call quickly. "For heaven's sake, it's time you called!" she scolded. "Just a text to say you're married, and not another word? Where are you?"

"I'm in Seattle, at my condo. I was wondering if we could drop by this morning."

"By all means, come right along! I'll be waiting. Don't dawdle!"

Wes poured more coffee for her. "So I couldn't help but notice that you didn't specify that the other half of 'us' is not Jareth," he observed.

"Nope," she said. "That's an explanation I'd prefer to make once, in person."

"Fair enough," he agreed.

It didn't take long to get through the late-morning traffic to Aunt Elaine's gracious Victorian mansion in Windermere. Ronnie loved the place far more than her father's house. All her happy childhood memories had been formed at this house.

They parked in the big, round driveway and they

walked through the garden, past the leaping fountains, the manicured flower beds. Wes looked strained.

"Relax," she told him. "She'll be disposed to like you. You're singlehandedly rescuing her from the consequences of her own silliness, to say nothing of mine. And what's more, you're not Jareth. She'll be easier to win over than my cousins."

"Why is that?" he asked. "What would your cousins have against me?"

She snorted. "You're a man, that's what," she said. "They're suspicious of any man who shows an interest in me or Maddie. They have this thing about protecting us from evil predators. It's sweet of them, but it gets tiresome."

The door was opened by Lizette, the tall, slim fiftyish woman with black bobbed hair who butlered for Aunt Elaine. Ronnie embraced her warmly. She'd known Lizette since she was fifteen, since the last butler retired, and she'd always liked her.

"Welcome back!" Lizette said. "You look wonderful. Mrs. Moss was so delighted about you visiting this morning. She's waiting in the library. Who's your friend?"

"Lizette, this is Wes Brody," Ronnie announced. "My husband."

Lizette blinked, nonplussed. "But aren't you…? Didn't you…?"

"No," Ronnie said. "There was a last-minute change of plan."

"Welcome!" Lizette recovered her professional aplomb quickly and shook Wes's hand. "I tell you what, Ronnie. I'll let you introduce your own husband to Mrs. Moss. I'll just get the coffee and cookies ready."

Aunt Elaine was sitting in state in the library, in her

favorite wingback chair, the one with a view of the portrait of her husband, Ronnie's uncle Bertram. Elaine
looked over with a big smile—which froze when she
saw Wes, and not Jareth.

She got up with the help of her cane. "Ronnie, darling," she said. "I assumed that you were coming here
with your husband, so that I could congratulate you.
Though I will not forgive you for cheating us out of
a proper wedding. A party afterward is not the same
thing, my dear. So where is your husband? And who is
this young man?"

"I'm not married to Jareth, Aunt," Ronnie said.

Elaine's face stiffened. "So your text wasn't true?
You're not married after all?"

"No, that's not what I said," Ronnie explained. "I am
married." She nodded toward Wes. "To him. Aunt Elaine,
meet Wes Brody. My husband."

Elaine's jaw dropped. "Good God, Ronnie," she said,
pressing her hand to her chest. "A little warning."

"Jareth refused to go through with it," Ronnie said.
"So Wes stepped in."

Aunt Elaine gave Wes a searching stare. "Well, well.
We owe him a debt of gratitude. Come on over here and
sit down, Mr....what was your name again?"

"Wes Brody. I'm glad to meet you, Mrs. Moss. Please
call me Wes."

"Then you must call me Elaine. Lizette is bringing
coffee and some of her marvelous Scottish shortbreads.
Settle in, young man." She leaned forward, patting the
chair next to her own. "Tell me all about yourself." She
smiled, but her eyes had a glint of pure steel. "And I...
mean...everything."

* * *

Over the next hour or two, Elaine Moss put Wes's nerves brutally to the test. When that woman said "everything," she meant everything. He told her about his past, his education, his mother, his work, his health history, his religious beliefs, his political stance, his knowledge of current events, his scientific literacy. Until his voice cracked.

The only facts she did not forcibly excavate were the details of his father's occupation. He mentioned that his father died when he was ten, and she had the delicacy to leave it alone. Random luck, because lying to her would not be easy, with those laser-bright eyes boring into his face. The woman would have made a kick-ass CIA interrogator. And all gracefully clothed in the guise of polite, friendly interest.

Ronnie watched the show, a subtle gleam of amusement in her eyes.

On the plus side, Elaine had shown no sign of recognizing his name. So Caleb and Tilda had kept the drama to themselves. It was a good thing that he hadn't pressed charges against Tilda for stealing the file. Everyone would have known his name. Ronnie would never have gotten anywhere near him.

But that wasn't the reason he'd passed on pressing charges. Truth was, he'd refrained because of Annika. He liked and respected Tilda Riley, though he'd been furious at her at the time. But she had done what she did for love, however dumb and wrongheaded it was. Not for spite, or revenge, or greed, or the other classic bad reasons. And she had a sweet little girl who would be motherless if Tilda got locked up.

He was a big sap, and he wasn't taking an innocent

little kid's mother away from her if he could help it. Mom and Dad would never have approved.

Lizette's coffee and shortbreads were a welcome diversion. He crunched one of the buttery, delicious cookies as he looked around the luxurious library. It was a large, bright, airy room, with high vaulted ceilings, and beautiful shelves of antique books. Portraits were hung at intervals between the bookshelves.

"Is this the family portrait gallery?" he asked.

"That's right," Elaine said. "This one is my late husband, Bertram." The old lady gestured at a portrait of a stern, handsome man in the prime of his life.

Then she pointed at a black-and-white photograph of a beautiful young dark-haired woman on a swing. "That's a photograph of my late daughter Susanna. Caleb, Marcus and Maddie's mother. I never had a chance to get a portrait painted of her. She never stayed still long enough. She never married, but she brought her children home for me to raise."

Wes recognized the subject of the next one. A striking painting in oil of a stunning redhead. He turned to Ronnie. "That one is you, right? It's amazing."

Ronnie shook her head with a little smile. "That's not me."

"That's Naomi," Elaine said. "Ronnie's mother. Uncanny, isn't it?"

"She could be Ronnie's twin," Wes said. "She's stunning."

Ronnie gazed at the portrait. "Hah. I know about your gift for blarney."

"Not about this," he said. "I could not overstate your beauty if I tried."

"I agree." Elaine gave him an approving look. "And

that's not all she got from Naomi. Her mother was a brilliant scientist and an innovative thinker. She was kind,
compassionate, principled. All good things. Veronica
inherited them all."

"I'm a lucky man," he said.

"You certainly are." Elaine looked at Ronnie. "You'll
want to take this portrait to your own home when you
start a dynasty. It's a precious memento of your mother."

"Ah, yes. About that," Ronnie said. "Aunt Elaine, Maddie said that she once went with you to a storage unit in
Greenwood where you kept some of my mother's things."

Elaine's brows rose. "Oh. Yes. I meant to tell you
about that, many times. But either you were rushing off
to the four corners of the globe, or Jerome was breathing down my neck. There was always something, so I
never got around to it."

"It seems pretty important," she said, keeping her
tone gentle.

"Well, not really," Elaine said. "You see, I went
through it. Truth to tell, there's not much there. At least
not much that has any relevance. I remember some
dishes, some furniture. Clothes and shoes, decades out
of date. She sent a container off on a slow boat before
the bombing happened. I picked out anything that might
have some personal meaning for you. Letters, photos,
jewelry. I think we got the best of it already. The rest
doesn't amount to that much. It's just odds and ends,
sweetheart. I stored if off the property to keep Jerome
from sniffing around and finding it."

"I'd like to look at it, if you don't mind."

"Good heavens, of course not. It belongs to you, of
course. I'm sorry I didn't tell you about it. Excuse me,

and I'll get the key for the storage unit right now. I have to dig around a bit. Back in a tick."

Once Elaine left the room, Wes sagged in his chair. "Whoa," he said fervently. "She is a piece of work."

"Yes, she's something," Ronnie agreed. "She definitely likes you."

"Likes me? I've been wrung out like a dishrag! How would I feel like if she disliked me?"

"She wrings us out, too," Ronnie assured him. "I think she's relieved. She and I acted in anger after my father misbehaved at Maddie's wedding, with that decision to put me into the mandate. When we cooled off, we both regretted it."

"Yeah? What did he do to deserve it?"

"Maddie and Jack had left the signing of the marriage certificate for the last minute, for dramatic effect. Right before midnight. My dad made the paperwork disappear before they could sign anything."

"Yikes," he said. "But clearly, his tactic didn't work. How did they pull that off?"

"They got privately married before the public ceremony," Ronnie said. "They left nothing to chance. Dad was beside himself. I haven't spoken to him since."

"Life is short," Wes said thoughtfully. "It's a shame, to be estranged from family."

"Oh, I doubt he misses me," she said. "But enough about him. I'm curious to see that storage unit, even if it's just dusty garbage."

"Hell, yeah," he said. "I can't wait."

Ronnie waved that away. "Oh, please. I don't expect you to root around in moldy boxes. You don't have to prove yourself to me. Go relax. I'll do it on my own and tell you what I find when I come home."

"I'm not letting you face those feelings alone. When I found my dad's journal, it was wrenching. I want to be there for you."

"Oh, that's lovely, honey! You should let him go with you! By all means."

They turned to see Aunt Elaine in the door of the library. "Sorry, love," her aunt said. "Was that a private moment?"

"Um…a little bit," Ronnie murmured.

"Oops. My bad." Elaine sounded unrepentant. "When a man offers to help with heavy, dusty boxes and possibly spiders, for goodness' sake, let him do it. What are men for, anyway?"

Wes choked on his laugher and stood, taking a bow. "At your service," he said.

"That's the spirit," Elaine said. "You'll do, Wes Brody."

"I hope so," he said. "She's incredibly special. She'll be hard to live up to."

Elaine's face softened. "I'm glad to hear you say that, and I hope that you mean it, because she is special. She deserves a man who's grateful. Jareth was never grateful, and that bothered me. Intensely."

"Aunt Elaine, please," Ronnie pleaded. "You're embarrassing me."

"Sorry, but I can't help it. It's what you deserve." Elaine locked eyes with Wes. "Buckle up, new guy," she said. "Whoever you are and whatever you've done, you will have to up your game to be worthy of her."

Wes inclined his head. The nod felt almost ceremonial. "I'm ready."

Elaine held out a small manila envelope to Ronnie. "That you go, darling. There's a key inside, and a card with the address of the storage place. Unit 824. I hope you find something that makes the trip worthwhile."

Ronnie took the envelope and tucked it in her purse. "Thank you, Aunt Elaine."

Aunt Elaine gave her a hug and turned to Wes. "And you," she said. "I hope you live up to your unexpected good fortune."

"Aunt Elaine!" Ronnie protested. "Give it a rest!"

"Oh, he can take it, honey," Elaine said. "I find that refreshing. He's sharp, too. Jareth was always too busy listening to himself talk to get my barbs. This one's different. He never misses a beat."

"I hope that's a good thing," Wes said wryly.

"It's certainly a more interesting thing." Elaine had a hint of humor in her voice. "I look forward to hosting dinner when all the kids get home. My goodness, what a gathering of talent that will be."

Wes forced a smile. "I look forward to it."

"And not that it's essential, but you are a fine specimen to add to our collection of ridiculous good looks," she said, with obvious satisfaction. "What a lineup. Something for every possible taste."

"Aunt!" Ronnie gasped. "That is so inappropriate!"

"Oh, pfft," Aunt Elaine scoffed. "I'm old and dotty, sweetheart. I get to be inappropriate when I feel like it. It's one of the very few advantages of advanced age."

They made their goodbyes, and got into the car, where Wes sat, staring blankly out the windshield at a hydrangea bush.

"Um…Wes?" Ronnie ventured. "Are you okay? Traumatized? Clobbered?"

He laughed and shook his head. "It was exhilarating. She's intense, but I like her."

Ronnie looked relieved. "Excellent, because she is important to me."

He concentrated on getting the car in gear before she could see the look in his eyes. He knew exactly what Elaine would think of him when the truth came out.

So now he had yet another reason to dread that moment.

They made their way to the Greenwood address on the card, Fillmore and Sons U-Store. It was a large complex, ringed by a chain-link fence.

At the glassed-in front office near the drive-through gate was a young woman with bleached blond hair and tattooed forearms. She looked up from her novel and her eyes stuck on him appreciatively.

"Excuse me," Ronnie said, her tone sharper than usual. "We need to get into unit 824. We have a key. Which way do we go?"

"Through this door, turn right, and go all the way to the last aisle before you turn left," the blonde girl said. "It should be halfway down that aisle."

It was starting to rain, and the wind was gusting hard, but they found the unit quickly. Ronnie stood staring at the door as if she were afraid of it. Gathering her courage.

Wes waited. The moment could not be rushed. Not with memories and ghosts rustling around them in the wind.

As if in answer to his thought, thunder rolled in the distance, and the rain got heavier, drops pattering down and marking the concrete.

She shot him a rueful smile. "Sorry," she whispered. "Just working up the nerve."

"Take your time," he said gently.

But as she fit the key into the lock, his own heartbeat sped up. His palms sweated.

Not cool. He could not display intense, inappropriate interest in the contents of Ronnie's mother's boxes. She would feel it, as intuitive as she was. And he did not want to ruin this. For him, or for her. It was too important.

He breathed to lessen his stress response as she pushed the door open.

Eleven

Ronnie stepped into stale darkness. There was a light switch by the door. She flicked it on, revealing a square, blank room, smelling of dust. A pile of boxes and a clump of plastic-wrapped furniture were positioned in the center.

There it was. She didn't know what she'd expected. She knew there would be no bolt of heavenly light from above, no angel chorus. So why the clammy hands, the racing heart, the butterflies? What the hell was she looking for?

Something to feed her hungry heart.

It made her feel so vulnerable, but at least Wes was with her. She could endure being seen in this naked, fragile state by Wes. Who knew why.

The rain was getting harder, so she stepped forward, making space for Wes to follow her in. She walked over to the stack, and around it. There were a few pieces of furniture. A plastic-wrapped wingback chair, the plastic long since decayed into shreds, thick with dust. A coffee table of a dark, carved wood that looked like it might be beautiful under the grime. Many larger boxes, some smaller ones.

They had all been opened and then resealed with packing tape. Presumably on Aunt Elaine's and Maddie's foray years ago, looking for photographs.

Her knees were wobbly, but this was a job that needed doing, with driving, focused attention, or else she'd drown in it. She seized one of the boxes on the top and tried lifting it. It was very heavy.

"Hey!" Wes said. "Hold it right there."

She looked at him over her shoulder. "Huh? Why?"

"Let me do the heavy lifting. Didn't you hear your aunt? What are men for but lifting dusty boxes and dealing with spiders?"

Ronnie laughed. "I'm actually quite strong, you know. I work out."

"I noticed," he said. "I've inspected every inch of you. I'm in awe."

"Stop your blathering. I also once wrote a paper in college on tropical arachnids. I'm not scared of a few barn spiders."

"Even so," he said firmly, hoisting up the box. "Indulge me. What does it cost you? One tiny, throwaway gesture, to make me feel useful and manly."

She laughed at him as she peeled off the tape that held the box closed.

It was full of books. Drip irrigation, hydroponics, ethical biofuels. Genetically modified seeds, the future of agricultural plastics.

"Let me open boxes at the same time," he suggested. "We can inventory them twice as fast. If I find something which strikes me as personal, I'll draw your attention to it." He reached into his coat pocket and pulled out a pen. "We'll label each box's contents when we're done."

It sounded like a plan, so they got right to it. She sat on the floor and went through the books in the box. Some pages were marked, notes taken in her mother's small, elegant cursive script.

She opened a book about drip irrigation techniques, and something fluttered down onto her lap. A bookmark.

Her heart jolted, in a flash of memory. It was a picture that she had drawn herself. The violets that had been blooming in the garden outside. She had tried to render the clump of flowers exactly, and then color it with her colored pens. Her dad's butler at the time, the benevolent old Mr. Braxton, had taken it to have it laminated so that she could send it to her mother in Sri Lanka as a bookmark.

Her mother had mailed her a similar bookmark, also laminated. A drawing Mom had drawn for her, of a Kadupul, the Queen of the Night. A beautiful, stately pink blossom with a yellow center, native to Sri Lanka. She'd painted it with watercolors.

Ronnie had kept that bookmark tacked to the wall over her bed until she went to college. She still had it, tucked into the photo album with her pictures of her mother.

It took a couple of minutes for the blur of tears to clear from her eyes.

"You found something?" Wes asked.

She held out the bookmark to him. "A bookmark that

I made and sent to her when she was in Sri Lanka. Mr. Braxton, the butler, helped me laminate it."

Wes leaned over and took the bookmark carefully in his hand. "It's beautiful," he said. "You drew this when you were seven? It's incredibly detailed."

She started to speak, then gave it up, and worked on making her chin stop shaking.

Wes handed the bookmark to Ronnie and rested his hand on her shoulder. "See?" he said gently. "Already worth it. You reached across time, and she reached back."

Ronnie let out a soggy laugh. "Stop it. Or I warn you, I'll cry."

"It's okay to cry," he said. "I cried when I read my dad's journal. You'll feel better if you do. That's another gift."

Ronnie looked away as her face dissolved again.

After that little meltdown, they settled in. Box after box of file folders, project reports, documents, correspondence, all regarding the many agricultural projects that her mother had been overseeing at the time.

The next few boxes were full of glassware, dishes. Then there was a box of beautiful teapots. Some looked very old. She lifted out a silver-plated one, with spots on it that were worn thin and stained dark from age. It was decorated with semiprecious stones in claw settings and had a handle made of yellowed horn.

She turned it around in her hand, understanding why her mother had decided to ship it home. It felt good, to resonate to the same beauty that Mom had.

"I'll take this one home today, and brew some tea in it," she said.

"Great idea," he said. "Hey, look at these. It's been just books up to now, but this one has textiles."

Ronnie knelt and pulled out the one on the top, un-wrapping the plastic wrapping. It was a handloom piece, made of silk and delicately embroidered with a compli-cated pattern, all in shades of blue. "Pretty," she said, digging deeper. "These are gorgeous. I have to do some-thing with these."

And so it went. Many, many boxes of things which time had made irrelevant, mixed in with small, random treasures.

The rainy afternoon faded into twilight. By then, she'd set aside a couple of big boxes of things to take home. Some of the lengths of cloths, a gorgeous set of mother of pearl brushes, combs and a hand mirror, several in-tricately carved wooden boxes, a set of wooden animals, wrapped in brown paper, and tucked into the middle of a bunch of genetics journals. There was a piece of paper taped to the top, and "Ronnie-babe" written on it, in her mother's beautiful cursive handwriting.

Wes never complained, as twilight stretched into eve-ning. She got up, rubbing her stiff knees. Wes was peel-ing open a fresh box and leafing swiftly through the files.

"This must be crushingly boring for you," she said.

"Wrong. There is nowhere in the world I'd rather be right now." He pulled an envelope from the box and looked up at her. "Ronnie?" he said. "Look at this."

She hurried over to him "What did you find?"

He passed her a battered manila envelope. On the front, in black marker, was "Letters from Ronnie." It had a wreath of doodled hearts all around it.

Her eyes fogged up as she pulled out the sheaf of let-ters. "Oh, my God," she whispered. "I wrote every week, and she kept them all." She shuffled through them. "I started every single one with 'How are you? I am fine.'"

Wes leaned over to look at them. "I bet she loved getting these letters."

Ronnie traced the hearts her mom had drawn on the envelope with her finger. Such an offhand, thoughtless doodle. She might not have done it consciously at all. And it had taken on such a huge significance, twenty-three years later.

Throwaway moments, lost in time. As precious as pearls.

She felt Wes's hand on her shoulder. "Hey," he said. "I know you're very focused, but you should have a cup of tea. Or dinner. You haven't eaten since those shortbreads."

Ronnie snuffled into a tissue. "Neither have you."

"Okay, fine. I admit, I'm hungry. Shall we break for a while? Come back tomorrow? We can take the things you set aside with us."

"They're heavy. We can bring a cart on another day."

"Let me bring them to the car now. You need those little animals on your shelf tonight. That bookmark gets tucked into the corkboard over your desk, and you need that teapot, to brew some tea after dinner. Speaking of dinner. Shall we order out?"

"Great idea. Thai Dream is near my place. They're great. Do you like Thai?"

"Love it," he said. "My mouth is watering already."

"Look at their online menu, and order in the car as we're heading home," she suggested. "I have an account there, and they deliver quickly."

"Sounds great. Let's make a run for it. It's still raining hard."

They made it out to the car getting only minimally soaked. Ronnie put the heat on while Wes took charge of ordering what sounded like a delicious and abundant meal from Thai Dream. The food arrived right after they got home. Wes carried up her boxes while Ronnie received the fragrant, heavy bags filled with Thai Dream's bounty. The timing was good because the rain had begun to pound very heavily.

Once inside, they set the table and popped open ice-cold beers. They feasted on dumplings, skewers of chicken with peanut sauce, rice noodles, grilled sea bass with a ginger sauce, beef and basil, curried shrimp, calamari. It was delicious. Reaching across time was hungry work.

Ronnie's smartphone buzzed as they were polishing off the calamari. She glanced at the display. "Excuse me, but this is one of my team," she told him. "I need to take this. Word must be getting around about the show being canceled."

"Go right ahead," he said. "I know there's a lot going on for you."

She hit Talk. "Hi, Elliott."

"Is it true?" Elliott wailed. "Are they insane?"

"Yes, they are, and I'm so sorry," she said. "Jareth and I didn't get married after all, so he canceled me out of spite."

"But it was so good! And everyone was making money hand over fist!"

"Yes, I know, I know. It's awful."

"We have to see if we can take it to another production company," Elliott said. "Avery and I are hopping on an early flight to Seattle. We made an appointment with an IP lawyer that Jane recommended. She's already studying our contract with Fadden Boyle, and she'll meet with us tomorrow afternoon at one. Can you be there?"

Her eyes strayed to Wes, hesitating for a second. "Yes, of course."

"Great. I'll text you the address. I think it's walking distance from your condo. Let's meet at noon, for coffee, before we go up to see her. There's no time to waste. I would hate to lose *Secret Life*'s momentum."

"Fingers crossed," Ronnie said. "Till tomorrow, then, Elliott."

She laid the phone down. "I have to leave you for a few hours tomorrow," she said. "My team wants to strategize. We're talking to an IP lawyer."

"Excellent," he said. "Don't worry about me. I've got plenty to do. I'm a big boy."

"You certainly are," she murmured.

They locked eyes, and she gazed straight at him, savoring the delicious hum of sexual tension between them. God, how she loved that. The intense awareness. The heat, rising. The mind connection, shining in the air. The hunger, growing, deepening.

Wes stood and went to the boxes that he'd carried inside. He took out the silver-plated teapot, and carried it to the sink, rinsing off the dust, and polishing it with a tea towel. Ronnie searched through her tea drawer for the jasmine tea and put the kettle on.

They brewed tea in the beautiful little pot, drinking the fragrant, steaming brew out of the delicate, gem-studded silver cups.

"The teapot looks good in here," he said. "I'm glad you have it."

"Yes, it's wonderful," she said. "Thank you, for encouraging me to do this. It feels incredible, to have her things around me. Like being kissed."

His smile was very sweet. "Anything that makes you feel good is all right by me."

Ronnie grabbed his hand. "You helped me make the leap. You know how it feels."

His eyes were somber. "You're welcome," he said. "It's an honor to be of service to you. Like I said to your aunt. I meant it."

She couldn't seem to speak, so she squeezed his hand.

"Trying to live up to you will make me a better man," he went on.

That made her intensely self-conscious. "Come on, Wes. Now you're overdoing it. I'm not some celestial being. I'm very fallible."

"I am not overdoing it." He lifted her hand to his lips, pressed slow, deliberate kisses to her knuckles. "It's straight from the heart."

The air turned electric. All she heard was the rain outside, a thrum against glass. She could hardly breathe for the shimmer, the ache of anticipation that glowed in every part of her body. It deepened, wanting to burst open like a flower and be entirely known.

Maybe she pulled him, maybe he pulled her, but soon they were twined together. Hungry, eager, pleading, demanding. Both ready to give everything to the other. Both demanding everything in return.

Such contradictions. She didn't know him at all, and yet, he knew her better than anyone ever had. After two days, she felt more real and authentic with him than she ever been before. She loved feeling so spontaneous, passionate, joyful, sensual. Bold and brave. Even…happy.

Oh, God. She was almost afraid to think it. Definitely afraid to feel it.

Wes lifted her up, her arms around his neck, her legs

around his waist, every part of her melting hot with pleasure, every part that touched him coming wildly alive.
She lifted herself, moving against him as he carried her
into the bedroom, cupping her bottom.

He kicked off his shoes before setting her down, pulling aside the bedclothes. The skylight over her bed was
a heavy drum of rain. The sound felt cleansing.

She pulled her clothes off, as he did with his own,
and pulled him on top of her, kissing him eagerly while
he caressed her most sensitive flesh with his incredible,
unerring skill, delving into her, slowly stroking. Just
the right spot, just the right way, swirling and pressing,
pushing her closer and closer to…oh yes.

The whole world was lost in a long, blinding pulse
of pleasure.

When she gathered her senses into one place, Wes
was on top of her, inside of her. His warmth covered her
whole body. Inside her, poised and waiting.

She gave him a lazy smile of encouragement, arching her spine, canting her hips.

"What are you waiting for?" she whispered.

"For you to say that," he said, laughing.

And they were off. Deep, slick, marvelous. He surged
inside her, as she clutched his shoulders, legs folded high,
nails dug into his shoulders, gasping. Egging him on.

He brought her to orgasm three more times with his
masterful skill, explosive and deep and wrenching. After
the third one, she drifted back to him kissing her forehead, his hand cradling her head, stroking her damp hair.

"Can I?" he asked, hoarsely.

"God, yes."

He let go, and so did she, clutching him and sobbing

as they launched over the edge. Soaring together, end-lessly.

Afterward, they got rid of what clothing clung to bod-ies and arranged the covers over themselves. It was all they had the strength for.

Then it was just cuddling. Lazily kissing, stroking, exploring, memorizing. Holding each other, as close as they could.

She draped herself over his big body, playing with his chest hair. Every detail of him was something to be mar-veled at. She had never been so relaxed. Images drifted through her head, of the day's discoveries. The book-mark, inside drip irrigation techniques. Doodled hearts on the envelope. The teapot, the wooden animals. Small things, seemingly insignificant, but they were caresses from an invisible, benevolent entity.

As a little girl, she'd liked to imagine that her mother was watching her from heaven. Or perhaps was even closer, like a ghost. As she got older, her rational mind had decided that fantasy was childish and silly. She'd locked it behind a heavy door.

But she hadn't killed it. It was alive, and as soft and open as she felt, that heavy door would not stay closed. It was wide open, and astonishing truths were rushing out.

That anything was possible. That love was eternal.

Maybe Mom had helped bring Wes to her so that Wes could bring her back to Mom. So many memories were waking up. The love she'd felt, the feelings she'd bur-ied, the loss, the pain. A heart hurt when it came back to life. It burned like a coal, but it was worth the pain. As the rain pattered gently on the glass above them, as she inhaled Wes's hot, salty scent, her face against his chest, she no longer felt afraid of it. That was Mom's gift to her. It would shine inside her forever.

Maybe. In any case, it was a lovely fantasy, and it hurt no one.

She let it carry her gently away.

Twelve

Nothing. There was nothing in Naomi Moss's boxes that pertained to the toxic-mold disaster or the subsequent cover-up.

His mother had pounded away at MossTech and their army of lawyers for years. Peg Brody had raged and railed until she exhausted herself, but the case against his dad had been watertight.

Or rather, it had been until Wes found the file, and his dad's journal. Over a decade after Mom's death.

Wes set the final box down right where they had left it the night before and stretched, wiping his hands on his jeans.

He'd marked the boxes he'd searched the day before. Today he'd gone through every box that he hadn't gone through himself yesterday. Page by page. Item by item.

There was nothing in this storage unit that could exonerate his father's memory or incriminate the senior Mosses. And all he felt about it was intense relief. That burden has been lifted from him. He would get no justice for his dad's disgrace, or his mom's heartbreak—that was true—but at least he was not obliged to attack the Moss family.

That would have killed him inside, now that he was bonded with Ronnie.

Of course, his love affair with her was doomed. The truth would come out as soon as Tilda and Caleb came back. He was screwed, no matter what he had or hadn't done.

He wished he'd never found his dad's journal and the lab notes in the Colombo house. That he'd met Ronnie Moss at some investor function or other and chatted her up like a normal guy. No agenda other than desire. Free to woo her with all the skill and style and charm that he had in his arsenal. And if he got lucky, marriage. A real one. A life with her. A family, tough as that would be with two busy careers. In sickness and in health.

And of course, in honor and in disgrace, like the Brodys did it. Mom had never lost faith in her man, no matter how they slandered him.

He wanted that life with Ronnie so badly. As much as Fate would allow. His parents had been cheated of that, and now he'd cheated himself of it, too. His dad's disgrace had tormented him all his life. He'd hoped that putting it right would give them all peace.

But everything had its price, and the price of his quest for truth was Ronnie. The sweetest thing life had to offer him. And oh God, was he sorry.

Now all that was left for him to do was to find the

courage to come clean. The last thing he could give her. Brutal honesty.

He shook out the kinks, and switched off the light, then locked up with the key he'd copied. Ronnie had left it on the kitchen bar, luckily for him, because he would not have the stomach to fish in her purse for it. Not that swiping a key that had been left in the open was any less a betrayal. But there were lines he wouldn't cross.

He strolled past the front office and heard a voice behind him. "Hey, Mr. Moss?"

Whoa. That whipped his head around. "Are you talking to me?"

"Yeah!" It was the blonde girl, coming to the door of the glassed-in front office. She wore short sleeves today, leaving the tree tattoos on her arms on full display.

"My name's not Moss," he told her.

"Oh." She looked confused. "But you're unit 824, right? Moss is the name on it."

"Yes, that's correct," he said. "It belongs to Veronica Moss."

"Okay. I just need to tell everyone from unit 820 through 836 that we had a problem with the rain gutters clogging the drain after the storm last night, and there was a little flooding this morning. Was there any water in your unit?"

"Just a trickle near the door. I swept it out into the drain outside. It didn't get near the boxes."

"Okay. I was just told to call and let everyone know that the problem has been fixed, and the gutters are clean. Will you tell her?"

"Sure. Thanks, I appreciate that."

He got into the Mercedes SUV that he'd leased that afternoon, after their leisurely brunch at Café Kuna.

One hand feasting on eggs Benedict and strawberries with cream, the other hand twined with Ronnie's slender hand, which needed an engagement ring.

Pearls, definitely. Glowing with the magic and the mystery of the sea.

It was money down the drain for sure. A foolish sacrifice upon the altar of guilt. When the truth came out, she would throw that ring in his face, and he would deserve it.

But he wanted to honor her with a ring worthy of her beauty. He wanted that moment with her, no matter what came after. He still hoped that somehow, he could convince her that his feelings were real, and the ring was tangible, costly evidence of his sincerity. Or maybe it would just look to her like more crass manipulation.

Screw it. He'd blunder forward in the dark as best he could. With a ring.

After a day of reading all of Naomi's correspondence, articles, reports, he'd concluded that the woman was just how Elaine had described her: intelligent, principled, committed to her work and to being of service. He liked Naomi Moss. She was a dedicated scientist, a devoted mother, a loving wife.

His father's journal had documented his confusion. He'd liked Naomi, too, and he hadn't wanted to believe that she could be behind that cover-up. He'd steeled himself to do the right thing if she was a criminal. Wes had memorized those passages.

Confronted Naomi M. today and demanded the truth. She promised to tell me everything, but only in person. Won't talk on the phone. Seems paranoid. She's sending copies of the documentation home in case something "happens" to her. Can't wait to be done with this crap and get back to Wes and Peg. I am not cut out for intrigue.

After what Wes had read today, he doubted that Naomi Moss had framed his dad. It was a shame that he couldn't have obtained this game-changing information before he'd ruined any possible future with Ronnie, but at least he wouldn't be throwing mud on Ronnie's memories of her mother. He of all people knew how bad that felt.

And despite her bossiness, he liked Elaine Moss. She'd been half a world away, running a far-flung company with her husband, raising three rambunctious grandkids. She'd been in no position to fabricate a frame job, or plot John Padraig's downfall.

He had to let go, and hope that his parents would forgive him. He was sure that they would, if they knew how he felt. Both of them were gone. He couldn't help them, or save them. There was no peace to be found by following this path. He couldn't change the past.

But dammit, he wanted a shot at the future.

So he was letting this go. He actually was. Damn.

The realization made him giddy and disoriented. Everything was changing. The ground shifting under his feet.

Tonight, he'd cook Ronnie a fabulous dinner. Then, he would book a room in the most beautiful and romantic place that he could find that was within a couple of hours' drive of the city. Tomorrow, he'd shop for the ring. He would present it to her once they were at their destination, and throw himself on her mercy. There had to be a way to make her understand.

He loved her. He wanted a life with her. He wanted to

offer her everything that he had, everything that he was. He'd do anything, give up anything for her.

Even his obsession for justice.

Thirteen

Ronnie had just parked her car when her smartphone buzzed. Lizette's name was on the display. Her aunt's butler.

"Hi, Lizette. Is everything okay with Aunt Elaine?"

"Everything's fine," Lizette said. "This isn't about Mrs. Moss. She's doing well."

"Great," she said. "So what's up?"

"Well, I got to thinking. When I heard that you'd asked for the keys to that storage unit, I remembered a conversation that I had years ago with Braxton, before he retired. It was at some big family event, maybe Christmas, and Braxton hinted about how Jerome went off the rails after your mother died and burned all her things. Papers, photographs and what have you. Braxton disapproved of that tantrum very strongly."

"Yes, I remember that tantrum," Ronnie said. "All too well."

"Well, anyhow, Braxton hinted that he hadn't let Jerome find everything. He'd kept some things aside that Jerome didn't know about. Braxton died a couple years after they hired Olsen, and Olsen might not have ever known about these things Braxton was keeping for you. So I called him yesterday, and I asked him to take a look in the nooks and crannies where a butler might hide a stash. And he called me back. He found it!"

"Oh," Ronnie said, her heart thudding. "Oh, my goodness."

"I know, right? So anyhow, call Olsen. He's very pleased with himself."

"I will. Thank you, Lizette. It's so nice of you to chase that down for me."

"Honey, it's my pleasure. I'm glad that my inquiry bore fruit. Tell me more when you find out what it is. Come visit and bring that lovely tall drink of water with you."

She laughed. "Will do, Lizette."

She sat there, a fine tremor of excitement and emotion vibrating through her.

Signs and symbols were gathering around her. She was trained in science, and didn't usually indulge in magical thinking, but right now, she felt as if she were in one of those ancient folk tales. The orphan girl with the magical tree that rained down gifts.

Someone was watching over her. Someone who loved her.

And what did it matter? Real or not, fantasy or not, she would just enjoy it and be grateful. To whatever or whoever was showering her with love and luck.

Olsen picked up on the first ring. "Veronica! Hello! I'm so glad you called."

"Hi, Olsen. Lizette told me you had found a box of my mother's things?"

"I did! In a crawl space up in the attic. A beautiful carved wooden chest, full of your baby things, and photographs. It has Veronica carved into the top. I would never have found it in a million years if Lizette hadn't told me to look for it."

"I'll come by and pick it up. Could I swing by tomorrow?"

"Of course. I'll be here, waiting for you."

She practically floated up to her condo. Delicious smells met her nose as she walked inside, and music was playing. Roddy Hepner's new hit single, "If You'd Only Take A Chance On Me." She set her purse on the shelf and entered the kitchen.

Wes smiled over his shoulder from the stove. "Good timing," he said. "I just decanted a nice pinot. It's been breathing the last few minutes, waiting for you." He set aside the wooden spoon, poured a glass of wine and handed it to her. "Try this."

Ronnie sipped it with a sigh of pleasure. "You've been busy."

"Oh, yeah. I leased a car, and I did some shopping and cooking. I also hatched tentative plans for a romantic honeymoon adventure. Pending your approval and availability, of course."

"I'm intrigued," she said. "Tell me more."

"I will, but first, come and have some dinner."

He ushered her into the dining area, and she gazed around with delight at the spectacle. Candles flickered on the table. A spike of calla lilies was the centerpiece, and a spread of goodies was laid out on many plates. Sliced cheeses, tiny little fresh mozzarella knots, plump red olives, sun-dried tomatoes and roasted eggplants.

"Sit down. Relax with your wine. Start nibbling while I drain the *paccheri*."

Ronnie did as he suggested. She hadn't eaten for a long time, and the wine was perfect. Everything looked and tasted fabulous. There was hot, crusty bread to go with it. A fresh salad, gleaming with olive oil.

After a couple minutes, Wes carried in two plates heaped with fresh *paccheri*, like big, floppy fresh macaroni noodles, chewy and delicious, dressed with a creamy, orange pinkish sauce, sprinkled with basil and grated pecorino cheese.

"We'll start with this while the steak is resting," he said.

"It looks wonderful," she said. "What's in that sauce?"

"Roasted red and yellow peppers. Once they soften in the oven, I peel and deseed them, sauté them with garlic and butter, and then purée and mixed them with fresh basil and some heavy cream. And the cheese at the end, of course."

She took a bite and moaned in bliss. "Wes, you're an artist."

"I know," he agreed. "I've always liked cooking."

The pasta was delicious, as was the tender grilled flatiron steak, the salad. To finish was a tiny, heart-shaped cheesecake, perfect for two, decorated on top with gleaming raspberries, blueberries and blackberries. "This, I bought," he admitted. "I didn't have time for pastry tonight. But I'm equal to it. I make a Christmas bread pudding out of gingerbread that would blow your mind.

Cream sauce with a slosh of good whiskey in it. My mom's holiday request, every Christmas. It was her favorite."

"I can't wait to taste it," she told him. "I'm not much of a cook myself. Eggs and toast and a sandwich, at best. Takeout and yogurt, usually. And fruit."

"Only the most delicious morsels shall pass your rosy lips when I am at your side."

She was charmed by his nonsense. It was seductive, being met when she came home by food, warmth, music, welcome. A glass of wine, a kiss. Someone who was happy to see her. It was an exquisite luxury. Some part of her felt like she didn't deserve it. She didn't dare let herself get used to it. Too sweet to be real. Too good to be true.

"So how did it go today?" Wes asked.

She nibbled her cheesecake, trying to take the smallest bites she could, just to make it last. "It was good to see my team, but the situation doesn't look good. According to this lawyer, our agent wasn't aggressive enough at protecting my interests. The way our contract is worded, if Jareth and his production team feel like messing with us, they could block us from taking the show elsewhere."

"Even if they refuse to produce it themselves?"

"Even then. Even if they did, I don't want to work with Jareth. I don't want him responsible for my livelihood, or for him to have control of my creative projects."

"I'm tempted to have a little conversation with him myself. Just to clear the air."

"Don't you dare," she warned him. "Don't get near him. All this stuff has absolutely nothing to do with you."

"Okay, don't worry," he soothed. "I won't worry my pretty little head. I'll stay in my proper place with my hands folded. Pinkie swear."

"Oh, stop it."

He nudged his chair closer. "Let's change the subject to something more cheerful and frivolous," he said. "I have an indecent proposition. Have you got meetings planned with your team for the next few days?"

"Not until next week. Elliott and Avery had to get back to LA to finish some other projects, and then we'll meet in LA. I told them that I needed a few days to decompress."

"Awesome," Wes said. "Because there's this resort I found. It's called Cloud Top. Only a few guests at a time allowed. Each suite has a terrace out in front with complete privacy and a view of the canyon, with hot mineral water piped into a private tub sunk into the rocks. If we get there in time, we can watch the sunset, naked and sipping prosecco, up to our nipples in hot mineral water. Here, look at the catalog."

He slid a tablet toward her. Ronnie scrolled through the stunning photos. The brochure showed all the different rooms and the terraces outside, the pools of steaming water. There was a sense of infinite space, soothing silence, exquisite luxury.

"It looks magical," she said.

"Good, because I took the liberty of booking five days there. Just you and me, far away from the jabbering voices and the grabby hands. In perfect privacy."

"Um…wow."

"I know this is a big ask," he said. "You're a busy woman, and a whole lot of people want a piece of you. I won't expect all your attention all the time. But for the next few days I'd really love to get you all to myself." He paused, looking at one of the photos. "Besides, can you imagine the fun we could have in one of those hot pools?"

"Yes, actually," she said. "When were you thinking of leaving?"

"How about tomorrow, late morning? We could check in tomorrow afternoon and watch the sunset. Dinner in our room. A long, luxurious soak. Hours of kissing. Time to learn more about you. What you dream about, what you like, what you hate, what you want. I want more data. More time. More Ronnie. As much as I can grab."

"Actually, you had me at 'indecent proposition,'" she said. "It's a fabulous idea."

"Excellent. I have to take care of an errand in the morning before we go."

"I have a couple of things to take care of, too," she said. "I need to stop by my father's house. My dad's butler, Olsen, told me that he found a box of my baby things. I absolutely want to collect that, as soon as possible. Just to protect it from my dad."

"I'd love to see where you grew up," he said. "Part of my data-gathering project."

Ronnie stood, shaking her hair loose and unbuttoning the top button of her white silk blouse. "I've got some data for you to collect, Wes." She unbuttoned the second button. Then the third. "Are you taking notes?"

"No need," he said. "I couldn't forget a single detail if I tried."

Ronnie finished the buttons, the cuffs. Peeled off the blouse. Unhooked the bra.

"Ronnie," he whispered. "You're so damn beautiful. It hurts to look at you."

"Suffer, then," she said, keeping her voice light. "But don't you dare look away."

That got a laugh from him. He stripped off his sweatshirt and she almost purred at the sight of his naked torso. So solid, so well proportioned. Too good to be true.

If something seems too good to be true, that's because it probably is.

Her father's cynical maxim floated into her head before she could block it. She wanted to slap it away, like a pesky fly. Or a wasp. This one stung.

And what was worse, there was a part of her that believed it. She'd always be carrying that doubt. A constant double vision. No matter how happy Wes made her, there was always that haunting certainty that anything so improbably sweet and fun and sensual and lovely had to be fleeting. Ephemeral. It was a natural law. Like gravity, like entropy.

It was the hard, painful stuff that stuck around, that stood the test of time. Guilt. Anger. Sorrow. You could count on those. They were as faithful as the dawn.

And so? Was that any reason to hold back? Life was short. Wes was here, right now. Tossing away his pants, standing there, stark naked, fully erect. Smoldering at her.

Now was not the time to pout about the ephemeral nature of love. Now was the time to take her satisfaction. She stepped out of her heels and shucked her pants. Snagged her panties with both thumbs and stripped them swiftly off.

Then she tossed away her comforter, and stretched out on the cool sheets, naked. She gazed up at him with sultry eyes. "Get over here, you," she said huskily.

He lost no time in obliging her.

Fourteen

"May I look at this one?" Wes asked.

"Certainly." The jeweler's eyes sparkled as she passed the pearl ring to Wes to examine more closely.

Yes. This was the one. It was a narrow platinum band with pavé diamonds all the way around, adorned by three natural pearls, each of a slightly different size. One was faintly pink, one was a rainbow-tinted, iridescent gray and one was a glowing, bronzy gold tone. A delicate ribbon of platinum studded with diamond brilliants held them together like a ribbon. Elegant, stunning, unique. Perfect for Ronnie.

It was also wildly expensive, but hey. If ever there was a time to make an extravagant statement, this was it. And he had plenty of money. What the hell.

The plan was to get Ronnie up to Cloud Top, soften her up with steaming mineral water, a sunset and champagne. Then he'd get on his knees, offer her the ring. Along with his heart, and his soul. He would blurt out the whole ugly, ungainly truth about his quest for justice. The lengths it had brought him to.

Of course, he couldn't buy a woman like Ronnie with a ring, or any sort of material goods. But symbols mattered. Sacrifice mattered.

He sized it on his own pinkie finger, having snooped into Ronnie's jewelry for just this purpose, just to be sure he was getting the size right.

Yes. It stuck exactly halfway up the second joint of his pinkie. Perfect.

"I'll take it," he said.

The woman beamed at him, as well she might, considering that she probably worked on commission. He'd looked at hundreds of rings today. He was lucky that he had a few points of reference. One, pearls. Two, a low setting, smooth, so as not to snag her nice cashmere knits. Three, it needed to be sublime. Gorgeous. Worthy of her divine beauty. The toughest requirement of all.

Once the transaction had been made, as well as the saleswoman's day—hell, probably her week—he tucked the small package into his bag and headed to his car. Everything was in place. Now it was balls to the wall.

The need to be honest with her had become urgent, driving. More painful with every hour he spent with her. He'd tell her how much he hoped for her forgiveness, her grace. The ring would say some of that nonverbally. The language of gemstones, held out by a man on his knees. Ring in one hand, and his naked, unprotected heart in the other.

Just take it. It belongs to you. Forever and always.

Please. Have mercy.

* * *

Oh, wow. Mom's textiles were gorgeous.

Ronnie sorted through the silk handloom and batik pieces that were packed into one of the boxes that they had left behind in the storage area.

An idea had come to her last night, while dozing in Wes's embrace. She'd been looking at his chest, focused on the cheerful bold pattern of her duvet cover that she'd bought from a catalog. She'd suddenly thought of the beautiful pieces of fabric art that her mother had chosen to take home. There were maybe fifteen or sixteen of them that she had counted so far. They would be fabulous duvet covers.

She'd picked out two for herself, and four more, one each for her cousins and one for her aunt. Maddie and Jack got one with all the colors of the changing ocean, a nod to Jack's ocean-cleaning-enzyme formula. Tilda and Caleb's had the colors of the sky: pale blue, dark blue, stormy darker grays, for Tilda's meteorological tool, Far Eye. Eve and Marcus got green, to honor Eve's Corzo project, which they all hoped would help feed the world. The fiery-toned sunset-colored one was for Aunt Elaine. For herself, the sunflower gold, and the peony pink.

It made her happy to imagine her house beautified by things that her mother had handpicked. Naomi, once again reaching across time, giving a subtle kiss to her grown-up daughter. It felt intimate. Fanciful, maybe, but she was going to indulge herself.

She packed the box. It wasn't heavy, just cloth inside. As she went out, she noticed moisture near the door, but she'd be cleaning this place out soon. The problem was barely worth addressing. She locked up.

The blonde at the front desk jumped up when she saw

her walking past. "Excuse me. You're Ms. Moss, right? The one with unit 824?"

Ronnie turned. "Yes, that's right. Can I help you?"

The blonde woman's eyes rolled in relief. "Okay, I was just checking, because I messed up yesterday, when I called your husband Mr. Moss, and I wondered if—"

"My husband?" Ronnie repeated. "Yesterday?"

"So, like, he told you about the leak, right?"

Ronnie felt bewildered. "Leak? No one told me anything."

The blonde woman looked dismayed. "I told him to tell you! There was a blocked rain gutter, and the water went under the door of some of the units. We fixed it, so it won't happen again. But I was supposed to call everyone."

"I noticed a little water, but it wasn't near the boxes. But my husband wasn't here yesterday. You must've mixed him up with someone else."

"Oh yes, he was!" the young woman said. "It was him. Pardon my saying so, but a guy like that makes an impression on the eyeballs."

"True," Ronnie said wryly. "But he couldn't have been impressed on your eyeballs yesterday because we were here on Tuesday together. Not yesterday."

"Nope. I know he was because I told him about the water damage. The rainstorm was Tuesday night, and yesterday was Wednesday, I crossed 824 off the list of units I needed to call about."

"That's strange," Ronnie said. "But don't sweat it. I'll ask him. In any case, I know about the leak, and it's no biggie. Have a good day."

"Okay," the girl said doubtfully. "Have a good day yourself."

Huh. Strange. Ronnie tried to put it out of her head. She went about her errands quickly, to the sewing studio, where she'd gotten some clothes designed. She laid out her specs for the larger pieces to be cleaned, restored and turned into six sets of king-size duvet covers, each one backed with a high-thread-count linen backing, made from the predominant color in each piece. An aqua blue, a gray, a dark forest green, a rusty orange, a pale pink, and a bright, sunshiny yellow.

But she enjoyed herself less than she should have while comparing color swatches, talking design, feeling closer to Mom. Because that interchange had been so strange.

Yesterday? How in the hell…? Maybe the blonde had just vaped something hallucinogenic on her coffee break. But something felt off.

She saw Wes's newly leased SUV was parked in front of her condo, and Wes met her at the door, with a sensual kiss. "Hi," she said, as soon as she could come up for air.

"Hi. I missed you. So I did my thing. How about you? We good to go?"

"I'm just bringing the bag I packed this morning." She'd just thrown in sweaters, active-wear pants and good shoes for mountain walks, plus sexy unmentionables. She hoped to spend the majority of her time wearing those items. Or nothing.

"Already packed into the SUV," Wes said promptly. "So that's all?"

"That's all for the luggage," she said. "There's just one thing I need to ask you."

"Ask away," he said.

"I stopped at the storage unit this morning, to pick a few things up," she said.

He looked distressed. "You should've told me. You know I like to be there with you, to help with carrying boxes and wrangling spiders."

"The box wasn't heavy, just fabric. I took them to be made into duvet covers. I want to give my cousins a set. A memento of Aunt Naomi. Plus one for Aunt Elaine."

"That's a great idea," he said. "They'll be beautiful."

"The woman at the counter says that she saw you there yesterday," she went on. "Evidently you guys had some sort of interchange about the water damage, which happened on Tuesday night. So…were you there?"

Wes frowned. "Yes, I was."

Ronnie's unease ripened into alarm. "Why on earth would you go there without telling me?"

He shrugged. "It's embarrassing, but yesterday after you left, I called about leasing a car, and when I went for my wallet for my credit card, I realized that I'd left my bag in the storage unit. It had my wallet, with my license, my cards, my cash. I didn't notice because I was carrying the boxes. You'd left the unit key on the bar, so I figured, why bother you? I called a car, went to the storage place for my bag, locked up and headed to the car dealership. I would have told you, but it was just logistics."

She relaxed. "Okay. I still wish you had said something."

"Sorry. I should have. I forgot. It would've come to me eventually."

"Okay," she said.

"So, next stop, the family seat. Lead the way. I feel like you're going to take us to some freaky Gothic pile on a windswept cliff. Or Bluebeard's castle."

She snickered. "That might be overstating it slightly. Dad's not a killer, just a garden-variety misogynist and curmudgeon. But he's in London, so our stop should be drama free. No telltale drops of blood, no one hanging by their hair in a locked tower room. Still, I want to rescue my box of keepsakes as soon as possible."

She looked into his smiling dark eyes and decided that she wasn't going to second-guess this. She'd milk it for all it was worth, not ruin it by being suspicious. Maybe she was a fatuous fool, but at least she'd be a blissful, happy, sexually fulfilled fatuous fool.

Fifteen

Wes was still shaking when they got on the road. Frantically wondering whether he had just hammered those coffin nails in even further by what he'd said to her.

More lies. But the timing was all wrong. He hadn't been ready, braced, fortified. He'd gotten so attached to the fantasy of going down on one knee at a luxury resort, pearl ring in hand. This was so delicate. It had to be carefully managed.

But he might have ruined everything. One more lie could be the final blow, if there had ever been any hope in the first place.

Ronnie's mood visibly altered as they got closer to her childhood home, as if a shadow had fallen over her.

"Are you okay?" he asked. "Are you sure that you want to do this right now?"

"Yes," she said. "I want everything that belonged to

my mother in my possession. I don't want to risk my father getting his hands on it."

They drew up to the tall, ornate wrought-iron gate, behind which was a stunning, ostentatious late-nineteenth-century mansion. Wes whistled softly. "Whoa."

"Yes, it's over-the-top," Ronnie said. "A rich, corrupt timber baron had this built as a wedding present for his extremely spoiled daughter at the end of the nineteenth century. She expanded it, and her children expanded again in the roaring twenties."

"It's impressive," he said. "But you sound like you don't approve of it."

Ronnie shrugged. "It's got bad memories for me. If I spend any amount of time here, I get depressed and anxious. This house will eventually be mine, I suppose. It'll go on the market before you can even blink."

"I hear you." Wes pulled the car to a halt.

A tall, balding man in his late fifties came out to greet them. Veronica greeted him warmly. "Olsen, let me present my husband, Wes Brody."

Olsen gave him a curious once-over. "I'm glad to meet you. Lizette told me about your news! I was so surprised. And…ah…Jareth?"

"Thought better of it," she said. "It's for the best. Wes suits me better."

Olsen grinned, pumping Wes's hand. "I'm so glad to hear that," he said. "Lizette spoke well of you. Come on in. The box is in the library."

The interior of the house was as spectacular as the exterior. Gleaming wood paneling, carved detailing, ornate molding, furnished with priceless antique furniture and fine art. Stained glass windows were in every room. The front hall had a beautiful Belle Epoque crystal chandelier. The grounds outside were exquisitely landscaped.

They were ushered into a huge library, with bookshelves that went up two stories high, colorful frescoes on the ceilings. A walkway stretched around the room halfway up, and sliding ladders were on both levels.

"What a room," Wes said. "It's stunning."

"Have a seat," Olsen encouraged, waving them toward the couch. On the table in front of it was a little beautiful wooden chest. Veronica was carved into the top.

Ronnie leaned over and touched it, her eyes shiny. "Wow," she whispered.

"I'll…ah…give you some privacy," Olsen said, hurrying out of the room.

"Would you like me to give you some privacy, too?" Wes asked gently. "I can wait right outside, if you want. For however long you need."

"No," she said swiftly. "Please, don't go. I want you right here with me."

"Whatever you want. I'm here for you."

She shot him a wan smile, then unlatched the clasp and lifted the lid.

The box was full of baby things, as Lizette had said. Ronnie lifted items out, one by one. White baby shoes, with satin roses. A white eyelet bib. A tarnished silver spoon. A crocheted lamb's-wool baby blanket. Onesies. A handful of small board books. She leafed through one of them, about a baby monkey who was looking for his mother.

She found an envelope full of photographs. Her as a newborn. Her at three months, four months, six months. Ronnie in her mother's arms, in her father's.

Ronnie held that picture up to examine it. "Huh," she

murmured. "I can't remember ever seeing that expression on his face when he was looking at me."

"How could he help it?" Wes asked. "You were such a cute baby."

She held up another one, of Naomi Moss leaning toward her husband, both of them hugging Ronnie, who looked about three. All of them were laughing.

"So there were some good times, back in the day," Wes said. "That picture wouldn't have been possible otherwise. Those smiles can't be faked."

Ronnie's eyes were wet. "I'm not sure if that makes things better, or worse."

"This is your mom, reaching out across time," he said. "I'm going to go out on a limb here and suggest that it's better. Things are trending better. Trust your mom."

She slanted him a look. "That's a sweet thought, but you haven't met my dad yet."

"You have a point," he admitted. "And I admit, I'm biased. I want things to be better for you. Not just better. The absolute best. You deserve it, and I want that for you with every fiber of my being."

He'd never been so sincere, or so terrified. So much hung on a thread.

Ronnie tucked the photos into the envelope. "Thank you," she said. "There are other treasures in here to pore over, but not here, not now. I can only take this house in microdoses, and I'm already over my limit." She shot him a teasing smile. "Besides, I'm excited to get to our romantic hideaway resort."

"Then let's be on our way." He hoisted up the chest. "I'll take this out to the car."

Olsen went before him, opening all the doors for Wes

on his way to the entry hall. Wes waited by the door as Ronnie gave Olsen a warm hug.

"Thanks so much for finding that box," she told him. "I know you must've spent hours crawling around in dusty hidey-holes looking for it. It means the world to me."

"I'm delighted that I did," Olsen told her. "I'm so glad that Lizette suggested it."

There was a thudding and a clatter outside, a shadow flickering outside the frosted windowpanes in the big front door, and the door swung suddenly open.

A sour-faced old man in a raincoat and hat stood in the doorway. His eyes narrowed as they fastened onto Wes.

"What the hell do you think you're doing here?" he growled.

"Dad!" Ronnie exclaimed. "I thought you were in London."

"I came back when I got the news." Her father kept staring at Wes. "I had to see what was going on with my own eyes. I certainly can't count on you to tell me the truth."

"That's unfair, Dad," Ronnie said. "What news? Who did you get it from?"

"You meant to keep it a secret, then?"

Ronnie sighed. There was no point in scolding her dad, or even fighting back. It just made things worse. Her dad never backed down, even when he was in the wrong. Which was always. "How did you find out?" she repeated.

"Jareth called me," he said.

That surprised her. "Jareth? I didn't know you two were engaged in any sort of independent dialogue."

"When it involves important information about you, we are."

Ronnie gasped, as it all came clear. "You got Jareth to screw me over in Vegas, right? I should have recognized your distinctive touch."

"Jareth isn't stupid, Veronica. He knew that my leadership at MossTech would increase its value by orders of magnitude. And after forty years of hard work and sacrifice, it was my turn to be CEO."

"Yes, and you would have taken MossTech public, which Uncle Bertram never wanted," she said. "Or my aunt or cousins. You'd just be making a group of rich shareholders richer."

"Stop mouthing off old platitudes," her father snapped. "It was refreshing to deal with Jareth. Finally, someone in the family who reasons with his head. So much for that, eh? What have we here?" He strode closer to Wes. "Who is this person?" he demanded. "Did you even bother to check? Or did you pick him because he was good in bed?"

"Watch it, Mr. Moss," Wes said. "No one speaks to my wife that way."

Her father's mouth twisted. "Do not scold me in my own house. What have you got there in that box? If you got it here, leave it here. It belongs to me."

Olsen stepped forward, his face grayish. "Sir, I assumed, since Miss Veronica's name was carved on the top of the box, that it belonged to—"

"You are wrong in that assumption, Olsen. Put it down!"

"No," Wes said, with steely calm. "The box is Ronnie's. You can't have it."

Her father's face turned red. "You son of a bitch. How dare you."

"It's just a baby box, Dad!" Ronnie yelled. "There is nothing that would be even remotely interesting to you! Baby shoes, blankets, onesies, board books! Just let me have it, for God's sake! What the hell do you care?"

"I thought I got rid of all that garbage," he said.

"Well, this one slipped through your fingers, and I am taking it," she told him.

Wes's gaze did not waver.

Her dad let out a grunt of disgust. "Fine. Take it, and good riddance. But that's the last thing you'll ever get from me. You're out, Veronica. You will not inherit a penny from me." He shot Wes a triumphant glance. "Not such a good bargain now, is she?"

"Holy God, Ronnie," Wes said. "This guy is unreal. Let's go."

"Yes, go on," her father sneered. "Run away. I'm sure that's exactly what you'll do, now that she's disinherited. Unemployed, too, from what I hear."

"So you agree with Jareth?" Her voice thin and colorless. "You think it's appropriate for him to cancel my show? Just to punish me?"

"Somebody has to," her father snapped. "You cruise along, doing as you please, never thinking of consequences. It's your aunt's fault. She always encouraged you."

"Thank God," Ronnie muttered. "Only reason I survived."

"And getting your name added to Elaine's mandate? You could have handed me control of MossTech, but no. You chose to give me your middle finger. And this person?" He gestured at Wes. "You look familiar. What's your name?"

"Weston Brody," Wes said.

"Humph. Don't know it." Her father scowled fiercely at Wes. "So you knew this man for what, two hours, before you married him? You're just like your mother. She couldn't resist the lure of sexual novelty either."

She opened her mouth to tell him what she thought of that, but Wes's gentle touch on her shoulder made her jump.

"Ronnie," he said. "There's no point. Don't even try. It's time to go."

She let out a slow breath and nodded. "Yes, you're right. Let's go now." She glanced at Olsen. "I'm so sorry about this," she said.

Olsen's face was tense, but he gave her a grave nod as he opened the door. "It's all right," he said, his face stoic. "Whatever happens. It's for the best."

They walked out to the car, ignoring her father's muttering and fuming.

Wes stowed the wooden chest carefully in the trunk. The silence was heavy as he drove. They'd been on the highway for forty minutes before she could speak at all.

"Wes," she said. "I'm so sorry."

"You're not the one who should be apologizing," he said.

"I let him get to me," she said. "Usually, when I interact with him, I'm braced for it. But today, he caught me by surprise. You'd think that I'd be used to it, right?"

"You should never have had to get used to treatment like that," Wes said. "He doesn't deserve to be near you."

"I doubt he intends to ever speak to me again," she

said. To her dismay, her chin started to shake. "Oh, dammit." She dug for a tissue.

"It's okay," he said. "You're entitled. I'd be trembling under the bed if I got treated like that by a parent. Who's supposed to love and protect and support you."

"Wes," she muttered, wiping her eyes. "You're not helping."

"Go ahead and cry," he said. "It's like taking a shower, but inside your head."

She followed his advice. Not that she had any choice. She turned her face away, and let the tears move through her. It exhausted her, and afterward, she drifted off.

She was pulled back to wakefulness by Wes's gentle touch on her shoulder.

"Sweetheart?" His deep voice was like the brush of silken fur. "We're here."

She stretched and yawned and looked around.

They were in another world. The trees so tall, the air intensely sweet, the colors so vivid. Every breath of chilly, pine-and-fir-scented air helped clear her muddled head.

The resort was like nothing she'd ever seen. The rooms were partly built into the rock shelf itself, as was the restaurant, which was cantilevered out over the canyon. It was a wonderland. Like being on Mount Olympus. A mythical landscape.

When they closed the door to their suite, Wes laid the wooden chest on the table, and followed her out to admire the view and the steaming pool of water on the patio a few steps below. The terrace was part raw, smooth stone, and part dark, textured gray slate. They were shielded on either side by thickets of sapling pines and firs. Only someone on the cliff across the canyon would ever see them, and only with binoculars.

"This place is incredible," Ronnie said. "I can't believe I never heard of it."

"It's new," he told her. "I only know about it because I invested money in it. It used to be the luxury hideaway of some eccentric software billionaire. He had a bad divorce, and the wife ended up with this place, so she sold it to a hotelier who turned it into a luxury resort. Speaking of luxury, the kitchen opens in a half an hour. Shall we go try out the Michelin-star chef? She specializes in fusion cuisine. After that, we retire for the evening. You and me, steaming hot water, moonlight?"

"Sounds great," she said.

A few minutes to freshen up, and they headed for the dining room, watching a spectacular sunset from the wall of windows, nibbling from a spread of gorgeous finger food. It was spectacular, but her appetite was off. She felt hollowed out.

"You're very quiet," Wes said. "Can I help? Can I do my clown act for you?"

"You can hardly help it," she told him, laughing. "It's hardwired into you. Oh, and by the way, thanks. For standing up to him. That was no clown act. That was a class act."

"Well, duh," he said. "Of course."

"Jareth always defended my dad," she said. "He would point out all the ways that it was my fault. Ways that I could be more compliant, more acceptable. As if I hadn't been trying for my entire goddamn life."

"Jareth is an ass-kissing, gaslighting troll. If I saw him, I'd slug him."

"No, you will not," Ronnie warned.

Wes mock pouted. "Aww. Can I key his car, at least?"

The phone buzzed in her purse. She pulled it out and gave him a pained look. "It's Dad," she said. "As if I would speak to him tonight. Like hell." She tapped the screen. "Decline. Take that, Dad."

"Turn it off," he said. "Take a night just for you."

"Don't mind if I do," she said. "I'll turn the ringer off. That'll show him."

She laid the phone on the table when she was done, nudging it away, and sipped her wine. "So, Wes," she said. "My fortunes have changed today. Does it make any difference to you that I've been cut out of the Moss inheritance?"

"Yes," he said. "As a matter fact, it does."

Whoo, boy. She hadn't expected that. Ronnie's belly clenched. "Well, thanks for your honesty, at least."

"No, no, you don't understand. It's the best news I've had since all this began."

"Excuse me? Exactly how could being disinherited be good news?"

"Because finally I can look you in the eye and say that I don't give a damn about the Moss fortune, and you actually might believe me. If you're disinherited and penniless, you can see that I'm sincere."

Ronnie laughed. "Silver linings, huh? 'Penniless' might be overstating it a little. I've saved money all these years of working, and I've bought property. And I'm definitely employable. Also, Uncle Bertram left me a few shares in the company when he died, so I'll never be destitute. But still. It's a huge step down, in terms of wealth."

"Who cares?" he said lightly. "I'm loaded, babe. Not that I really ever cared. It just happened, because I'm good at what I do. Plus, my small superpower is that

I'm not afraid of taking risks. That's because I genuinely never gave a shit whether I lost it all or not. But that's over for me. For the first time in my life, I've got something precious. Something that I'm scared to death of losing. I don't want to screw this up."

She seized his hand. "I can't imagine how you could screw this up, Wes."

"You're very generous," he said. "I hope you can continue to be generous when I end up…disappointing you."

She laughed, trying to lighten the moment. "Gee," she teased. "Do you have any immediate plans to disappoint me?"

"It's inevitable," Wes said. "It's a mathematical certainty. People are flawed. They mess up. They miss the mark. Though I can't see any flaw in you yet."

She squeezed his hand. "That's sweet, but it's only a matter of time. Of course I'm flawed. We all are. But today, you were my hero. Are you ready to go to the room?"

"Oh, God, yes." He leaned over the table. Their lips met, a sweet, searching kiss, so full of tenderness and exquisite care. One hand holding her hand, the other stroking her face as if he could hardly believe she was real.

She leaned into it. His kiss made her so soft and open, aching for him. She leaned back, gasping for air. "Right now," she said, breathlessly.

Sixteen

Wes's mind raced when the door to the suite closed behind them. Was this the big moment? The best moment? The ring was still in his bag, not in his pocket, and the bag was in the bedroom, and Ronnie was so sweetly passionate and on fire. He didn't want to interrupt the wonderful erotic momentum.

He wanted to worship her, pleasure her, persuade her. She was a miraculous creature, and he'd compromised that, and it just made him so…damn…*angry*.

"What?" She was panting. "What's the matter? Is something wrong?"

"No, no," he assured her. "It's wonderful. I'm just kind of emotional tonight."

Her expression softened. "Oh, me too," she said. "I'm glad that I'm not the only one." She pulled off her sweater.

They yanked off their clothes, eager for that rush of electric joy that went with skin on hot skin. Wes tossed the covers back on the bed and turned as Ronnie gave him a hard shove on the chest. He yielded to the pressure, pitching backward onto the bed, bouncing.

She climbed on top of him, her silky thighs clamped around his, her slender hands stroking his shaft, making him shiver and moan. She braced her other arm against his chest. Her radiant smile made his heart twist and burn with longing. Her hair draped around them like a fragrant satin curtain. She rained soft kisses on his forehead, his cheekbones. Too much. He couldn't be so close to her, so tuned to her, and not be completely honest with her. It was killing him. "Ronnie," he whispered.

"Mmm?" She stroked her velvety soft cheek against his, then kissed it.

"I have to tell you... We have to... Oh, my God, Ronnie."

She rose up, undulating over him, sliding and wiggling along the length of his shaft. Anointing him with her sweet, hot, wet balm. "Yes?" she asked sweetly. "You were saying?"

"I need to tell you...that...I...that...ah...oh God."

His voice trailed off, dumbstruck, as she reared up, nudging the tip of his penis inside her slick opening. Hot, clinging. She arched, poised for a long moment as the anticipation built...and then, slowly sank down and enveloped his aching shaft into the delicious, clutching heat of her perfect body.

And that was it. Couldn't speak or think. All he could do was watch the stunning spectacle of Ronnie Moss, moving over him. First slow, graceful, a sensual spectacle. Then it got more intense as she sought her own pleasure. Riding him, all the way to blinding completion. When the delicious clutching flutters around his penis eased, he rolled her onto her back, and lost himself inside her. Wild, wonderful, deep…then the explosion, wiping away his fear and dread. At least for that sweet, blinding instant.

They lay there, damp and panting. Relaxing as the sweat dried, and their galloping heartbeats slowed. And the dread crept in. It would not leave him alone.

Some time later, Ronnie disengaged herself, and disappeared into the bathroom. She came out moments later, winding her hair up into a knot, fastening it with a clip. She slid open the door at the patio. Puffs of steam rose from the pool and into the moonlit air.

"I'm going to soak in this pool and look at the moon," she said. "Join me?"

There was only one possible answer to that question. He followed her immediately, hypnotized by the beauty of her elegant, sinuous nude body as she paced around the hot pool, every line, every curve, painted by moonlight and shadow.

She stepped into the pool, descending to her waist. The sound of the water sloshing and trickling sounded incredibly sensual. She sank onto the bench with a sigh.

He followed her in, sinking down, drifting over to float right in front of her.

He was giving himself one more night of perfection. Tomorrow morning, he would tell her everything, and they would face reality together. No matter what happened.

He pulled her into his arms. This might be all he ever got of the shining miracle that was Ronnie Moss. He damn well better make this night count.

* * *

Wes ran as fast as he could along rocky, uneven ground. Pounding feet, heart in his mouth, life-or-death urgency, either toward something or away from something. A chasm yawned in front of him, immeasurably deep. He reeled, teetering. Couldn't stop. His momentum had pitched him over the edge, and he couldn't even see the bottom, it was so far below, lost in the mist. Rocks and dirt pitched off with him. He yelled—

A strong hand caught his wrist and pulled him up. Easily, as if he were only ten years old. It was his dad. His eyes looked worried as he set Wes onto his feet.

*Wes lunged to grab him...*but the light was pressing on his eyelids. When he opened his eyes, they were wet with tears.

He pressed his face to the pillow and looked around. The room was bright. The sun was well up. They had gotten to sleep late.

Ronnie wasn't in the bed. He sat up, looking around, and saw her cross-legged on the floor, sitting in a square of sunshine from the window. She wore a white, fluffy hotel bathrobe over her sexy teddy nightgown. Her hair streamed over her shoulders. Her mother's baby box was open in front of her. Small objects were arrayed before her, on a clean towel that she'd spread out onto the carpet.

She was holding up a tiny, multicolored knit baby jumper. A pair of miniscule pink socks. A hairband, with silk flowers on it. A black velvet baby coat. Tiny pink hair clips.

Wes got up, shrugging on his own robe, and went over to kneel next to her.

Ronnie gave him a smile, but her eyes were wet. "Hey

there," she said, her voice husky with tears. "Don't mind me. I'm just over here, yanking on my own heartstrings."

"I hope it's a good feeling," he said.

"Yes," she assured him. "It aches, but it also makes me feel loved." She held an object up to him. "Look at this. From the day I was born."

Wes examined it. It was two plastic ratchet-closed hospital bracelets, linked to each other. The big one had Naomi Moss printed on it, the little one Veronica Moss. Wes cradled it in his hand, as if it were alive.

"Beautiful," he said. "An artifact of love."

"Yes," she said. "Yes, exactly." She reached for a tissue, in the pocket of her robe, and blew her nose noisily. "I would never have found these, if not for you. And despite all the ugliness with Dad, it's just so healing."

Wes looked into her eyes, and it came into focus, in a blinding moment of realization. This was it. This was his moment. He would never have a better time to redress his mistakes. Never a moment when her heart was softer, her mind more open and disposed to forgive his transgressions. Never a better time to beg for mercy.

He had to man up and do this thing.

Right. Freaking. Now.

He went to the bag where he'd stowed the pearl ring, then crossed over to Ronnie with the box in his hand. He sat next to her on the floor.

"Ronnie," he said. "These last few days since I met you have been the best days I've ever had. In my entire life."

Ronnie dabbed at her eyes, smiling at him. "Me too."

"I know we're already married, so we skipped over the part where I try to convince you that I'm the man who should stand by you for the rest of your life. To make a family with. Grow old with. The whole thing. The real deal."

Ronnie blinked at him. "Wes…are you…um…?"

"Yes," he said. "I'm proposing to you. Sort of. Insofar as an already married man can propose to his wife. I want you with me forever. And I want you to have…this."

He flipped open the ring box and held it up, holding his breath.

Ronnie gasped. "Oh, Wes."

"Will you wear it?"

She nodded. He took the ring out and slid it onto her finger, nestling it up to the wedding band. The two rings together looked great on her.

"It's so beautiful," she said. "Pearls. You sneaky bastard."

"It looks perfect on you," he said. "But if you wanted to look at some other designs, I'm sure that the jeweler could swap it out with—"

"Not a chance. It's the most gorgeous ring I've ever seen. Look no further."

Wes let out a sigh of relief, and then took a fresh deep breath. "I'm so glad," he said. "Because there's another thing I need to talk to you about. An important thing."

"Yeah? So? Let's have it."

"Yeah. It's kind of hard to say. I'm nervous about how you're going to take it. And it's hard to find a place to start that makes sense," he said haltingly.

She grabbed his hand, squeezed it. "We have time. I'm not going anywhere."

God, he hoped that generous attitude would continue when he finally got to the point. "Thanks," he said, swallowing hard. "It's about my dad. How he—"

Rat—tat—tat—tat. A brisk knock sounded on the door, making them jump.

Goddammit. Wes's teeth ground. "Did I really forget to put the Do Not Disturb sign on the door?" he muttered.

Ronnie rolled her eyes and got up, pulling her robe closed and tying the sash as she went to the door. "Who is it?" she called.

"Ms. Moss and Mr. Brody?" It was a male voice behind the door. "I'm very sorry to disturb you, but I have a smartphone that one of you left in the dining room last night. The cleaning crew found it this morning. I thought you might want it."

"I believe that must be mine," Ronnie said, opening the door. She took the phone, murmuring her thanks to the hotel employee. She looked down at it as she closed the door.

"That explains that," she said. "I was feeling both grateful and puzzled that no one was bugging me today while I had my sentimental moment with the baby box. So I'll just switch this thing off, and you can tell me what you were going to…"

Ronnie's voice trailed off. She froze in place, staring at the phone screen.

Wes felt the energy in the air change, and a chill gripped the pit of his stomach.

"What?" he asked. "Is something wrong?"

"Six missed calls from my dad, five from Maddie, four from Lizette. Something's happened. None from Aunt Elaine. She always calls when there's a crisis. Not this time."

"Which suggests that Elaine herself is the crisis," he said.

"Yes. Excuse me, but I have to get back to them." She

tapped the screen, sitting on the bed. "Lizette? It's… Yeah. Sorry I didn't get back to you sooner… Oh God. When?" She pressed her fingers to her mouth, her slim shoulders hunched. "Yes, I understand. I'm glad they're on their way. Which hospital? Of course. It should take us two and a half, three hours tops, to get back to the city… Yes, of course. We'll come right away. Thanks, Lizette. I'm so glad you were with her."

Ronnie let the phone drop. She met his eyes. "Heart attack," she said, her voice strangled. "After dinner last night. They tried and tried to call me. She's at the University of Washington Medical Center. Having surgery. Right now."

She clapped her hand to her mouth, leaped up and bolted into the bathroom. He heard retching sounds. Then running water, as she splashed her face in the sink.

She came out, and plugged her phone in. "I'll get as much charge onto this thing as I can while I'm packing." She knelt, swiftly stowing all the baby artifacts into the wooden box. She gave him an impatient look as she jerked on her hiking pants and wound her hair into a quick braid. "Wes?" she said. "Please? Move!"

That jolted him out of his dismayed paralysis. "Of course. Right away."

He got dressed in record time, ashamed of himself. Feeling put-upon about his confession being interrupted when Ronnie's aunt was fighting for her life. But dear God, the timing. He couldn't tell her now. Her mind was consumed with worry for her aunt. Which was just as it should be. He'd waited too long.

All he could do now was grit his teeth and wait for another chance.

* * *

Ronnie spotted Maddie in the waiting room of the surgery ward. Her cousin met her with a tight hug. "I'm so glad you're here," Maddie whispered. "The boys are on their way home as fast as they can get here, and Jack's been here for me. And Jerome, of course," she added, a hint of irony in her voice. "But I wanted you."

"How is she?" Ronnie asked.

"Still on the table," Maddie said. "It's bad. Evidently her doctors have been planning this bypass surgery for a while, but she neglected to tell us about it. They're doing quadruple bypass and a valve replacement. Gran is as tough as nails, though. We just have to grit our teeth and hope."

"Sorry I didn't call," Ronnie said. "I left my phone in the resort restaurant."

"Resort, huh? Sounds festive. I'm glad you were having fun, at least, before all this happened. I'm so sorry to have interrupted the honeymoon."

"Are you kidding? Aunt Elaine is everything to me. We can honeymoon for as long as we like later on."

"Yeah, absolutely," Maddie agreed. "Jack and I decided that if it's a girl, she'll be Elaine. We'll call her Lainie. I'll tell her as soon as she wakes up. We were waiting for the ultrasound, but I'm not waiting for anything, ever again."

Maddie dissolved into tears, and they hugged again. Then she glimpsed her father approaching, over Maddie's heaving shoulder. Her belly clenched, bracing for whatever.

Wes moved closer, too. Instinctively protective. How sweet of him.

"Aww. How touching," her dad drawled. "Twelve

hours of radio silence, entirely ignoring all our frantic calls, and you finally deign to come to your ailing aunt's side."

"I didn't get the messages until today," she said.

Ronnie let them catch her up on all the details that the surgeon had shared so far. They took turns as the hours ground by, taking breaks for air, coffee, sandwiches from time to time. At one point, Wes accompanied her to the hospital cafeteria, but instead of getting in line at the bar, he took her arm and led her through the lobby and outside, into the chilly evening air, under the big porticos.

Wes squeezed her shoulders gently with both hands. "Ronnie, I know this is a bad time," he said. "But remember this morning? I was about to tell you some things that I think you should know about me."

"Oh, Wes. I'm fried and distracted right now. Let's just stick with the present emergency and save the reflections about the past for later. When I can give you the focused attention that you deserve. Forgive me for putting you off, okay?"

"I understand how you feel, but please." Wes's voice vibrated with tension. "I think it's important, to say this to you now. Even in the face of Elaine's emergency. Maybe especially in the face of it."

Ronnie sighed and nodded. "Okay. If it's that important, then let's hear it."

"I'll be quick." He grabbed her hands and kissed them. "Thank you. So, like I was saying this morning, this is about my dad. Twenty-three years ago, he was in—"

"Wes Brody?" They jerked their heads around, at the loud, accusing tone behind them. "What the hell? Get your hands off my cousin!"

Caleb and Tilda Moss stood there, staring at them.

Seventeen

So. This was the way it had to be. Wes let out a sigh as the certainty of his doom settled into his guts. He squeezed Ronnie's hands one last time, just in case it was the last time she permitted him to touch her and turned to face Caleb and Tilda. "Hello, Caleb," he said grimly. "Tilda."

"Wait." Ronnie's eyes were bewildered as she looked at them. "You guys know each other?"

"You could say that," Wes said.

"Yeah, I know this scheming son of a bitch," Caleb said. "He has no business touching you, Ron. He tried to attack MossTech with a faked file that implicated our family in a crime from years ago. Grandpa Bertram, Gran, Jerome. Even your mother."

Ronnie turned to Wes, horrified. "That can't be true," she said. "Is that true?"

Wes tried to swallow, but there was a burning lump in his throat. "It's complicated," he said. "It's true, I had a fact-finding agenda at the beginning. But as soon as I started getting to know you, that changed, and I started to—"

"No. No, stop it right there. I don't want to hear another word."

"Ronnie, please. I was trying to tell you. I tried this morning, before you made the call to Lizette. I tried again, just now."

"So that's why you encouraged me to find my mother's things," she whispered. "Not for the healing love, and her hand reaching out across time to caress me. It was so that you could snoop and pry in our family's private documents."

"Ronnie—"

"Oh God." She backed up a step. "All those tender moments. Completely faked."

"I never faked anything," he protested. "Not for one second."

"And the other day, you didn't go back to that storage unit to get your bag. You took my key, and you snooped through my mother's boxes. To hurt me."

"No," he said. "I would never hurt you."

"Bullshit! Every damn thing you've ever said to me was a lie."

"That's not true." He reached out, but Ronnie slapped his hand away. "I had to see if the papers were there," he said desperately. "I was looking for the documents that would exonerate my dad."

"Exonerate who? What the hell are you talking about?"

"The toxic-mold disaster," Wes said. "The one in the

file Caleb mentioned. It happened. People died. Someone tried to cover it up, and they blamed everything on my dad, who had died in the bombing. Along with your mom."

Ronnie's face was blank. "But I don't remember hearing about anyone named Brody," she said. "The name of the man who died with her was John Padraig."

"He was my stepdad."

"Stepdad?" Ronnie's tone was accusing. "What stepdad?"

"He was the only father I ever knew. I called him Dad. I was a baby when my mother met him. I was a mistake made when she was nineteen. Then she met my dad, and they fell in love. They intended to get married eventually, and he intended to adopt me and give me his name, but he never got around to it. Then time ran out for him. He died in that blast, and the whole mess got pinned on him. It broke my mom's heart."

"I see." Ronnie's mouth shook. "So you decided to break mine to make it even?"

"Absolutely not," he said forcefully. "Never."

"I understand wanting the truth," she said. "Ironic, though, that you sought the truth by lying to me. Continually. Even while we were making love."

Caleb and Tilda exchanged shocked glances. "What the hell is going on?" Caleb demanded. "And where is Jareth?"

"Jareth is history. He bailed on me. I married Wes instead. God help me."

"Oh, dear God," Tilda said, her voice small.

"Yes. Jareth and Dad planned it out, for him to choke at the last minute and make me miss the deadline. I thought it was all over." She gestured at Wes. "Then he happened along, seemingly by chance. He offered himself up to help me fulfill the mandate. So generous, right? All he wanted was the entertainment value and the pleasure of my company. You are a world-class liar, Wes. And I am an empty-headed fool."

"I wasn't lying," he said. "I knew I was screwed when you turned out to be the woman of my dreams."

"Oh, stop it. You're just doing your bullshit blather out of habit. It's not necessary to keep up the pretense anymore, so stop."

"Please, Ronnie," he said. "Try to imagine being in my position. If someone had accused your mother of horrible crimes, wouldn't you do anything to find the truth?"

"Don't speak of my mother again," she said. "You were digging for dirt in her private papers, to throw at her memory. Now you're asking for understanding?"

"I wasn't trying to hurt anyone," he insisted. "I just had to see if what was in my dad's journal was true. She told him that she'd copied her documentation and sent it home with her things, in case anything happened to her. Dad thought she was being overdramatic. That last journal entry was dated the day they both died."

"Where is this journal?" Ronnie demanded. "Can I see it?"

"No," Wes said. "Tilda burned it."

Tilda winced. "Wes, you should have told me all this. I had no idea your father was involved."

"The documentation in that file showed the cover-up," Wes said. "I didn't start questioning that until now. But my father didn't want Naomi to be guilty. He wanted to get to the bottom of it. I don't think she's guilty, either. Not anymore."

Ronnie brushed the backs of her hands across her

eyes, but they were still wet, glittering with shock and tears. "And why on earth would you change your mind about my mother now?"

"Because I read her letters," Wes said simply. "Naomi wasn't a venal, money-grubbing hack who didn't care about people dying from toxic mold. That was someone else. But not my dad."

"You still have that transcript, right?" Tilda said. "There was a printed transcript in the file copy that you gave me last year."

"Yes, but it doesn't hold up as proof," Wes said. "It just points to Naomi's shipment home. My last signpost."

"Oh God," Ronnie said. "So you and Tilda and my dad all knew about this file, and you never saw fit to tell me?"

Caleb looked pained. "I'm sorry, Ronnie," he said. "I thought it was better to just let it be. I didn't tell Marcus or Gran either."

"I'd like to see the transcript," Ronnie said stiffly.

Wes pulled out his phone, attached the file and sent it to her email address. "Done," he said.

"Forward it to Caleb and me, too, Ron," Tilda said.

Ronnie tapped at her phone, her mouth tight. "So I take it the other day, at the storage unit, that you did search my mother's things."

"Yes," he admitted. "Everything."

"And did you find anything incriminating or exonerating?"

"Nothing," he said. "Just evidence that she was dedicated and altruistic, and working hard. That she was far from home, and missing her husband and her little girl. I liked her."

"Don't," Ronnie said stiffly. "Those letters weren't yours to read. She isn't yours to like."

"I'm sorry."

He stood there, locked in misery while Ronnie blew her nose and squared her shoulders, staring at him with blazing eyes. "This wasn't a complete loss for you," she said. "You set your doubts to rest. You will never find anything else that belonged to my mother, so you have no reason to linger. I'm surprised you didn't disappear after you finished at the storage unit. Why drag out the charade? Were you just enjoying the sex?"

God, it hurt to breathe. "No, I stayed for you. I never wanted to leave you, ever again. I still don't. I'm sorry I didn't tell you sooner. I kept waiting for the perfect time, and I missed my window."

"There was never a window, Wes," she said. "There's never a good time to find out that you've been lied to and screwed over."

"I couldn't think of any other way," he said. "Not after what happened with Tilda and Caleb. But I've been regretting it since that first night."

Ronnie looked at Caleb. "I wish you told me this whole story," she said.

"I was trying to keep things calm," Caleb said. "Once everything was burned, what was the point of getting everyone all upset?"

"If I had known his name, I wouldn't have run into his arms like an idiot," Ronnie said.

"I'm sorry, Ron," Caleb said. "I never meant to hurt you."

"Neither did I," Wes said.

Caleb glared at him. "Shut up."

Wes ignored him, eyes locked on Ronnie. "I love you," he said.

Ronnie shook her head. "You're not credible, Wes," she said. "Just go. And for God sake, take this." She tugged the pearl ring off, and held it out, but she got tired of his refusal to take it. She grabbed his hand, and slapped the ring into his palm.

"What about the marriage mandate?" Wes asked. "Are you just going to give MossTech to Jerome?"

Ronnie gave Caleb a stricken glance.

"It doesn't have to be that way," Wes said. "Even if you don't want me near you, we can leave things as they are. Please. I want to do at least that much for you."

Caleb and Tilda gave each other a searching look, and in unison, shook their heads.

Caleb looked at Ronnie. "Cut him loose," Caleb said. "You can't continue with this marriage after what he's done. Not even at a distance. None of us would ask that of you, even if you were willing."

"I'm so sorry," Ronnie said. "I wrecked everything."

"It wasn't your fault," Tilda said. "You never deceived anyone. Let Jerome do his worst. We've all been braced to let MossTech go for months."

Ronnie turned to Wes, head high. "We're done," she said. "You'll hear from my lawyers about filing for a divorce. Goodbye."

She spun around, and marched back into the hospital, spine elegantly straight.

Caleb and Tilda might have said something before they followed her in, and they might not. He couldn't hear them over the roaring in his ears, and wouldn't have understood if he had. He just stood there and clutched the pearl ring so tightly, the diamond band practically carved itself into his palm. Trying to take it in. The doomsday, rock-bottom, worst-case scenario.

The worst of all possible worlds. That was the one he had to live in.

Eighteen

Four months later...

Ronnie shivered on the cot in the doctor's examining room. She'd been there in the chilly room for over forty minutes waiting for the bloodwork.

Her symptoms were annoyingly vague, and all of it could be attributed to stress. Blood pressure so low, she felt dizzy and queasy. Heartburn, short breath, swelling, spotty periods, waves of intense fatigue. She just felt... weird. Not herself. Probably just stress, from being miserable, hurt, humiliated. It was enough to drive anyone off the deep end.

At least Aunt Elaine was recovering. She was almost back to her former self.

Ronnie just hoped that whatever she had wasn't alarming. Aunt Elaine's heart attack was enough stress for now. Plus, she wanted to focus on happier things, like the babies. Tilda was pregnant, Eve, too. Maddie was coming right along, just two months to go. A whole crop of gorgeous Moss babies would soon be rolling around together on Aunt Elaine's fine Persian rugs. She didn't want to be the buzzkill lonely-hearts spinster aunt with the chronic health problems, angling for attention.

Stop whining. Crybaby. Suck it up.

Her dad's voice in her head. She should not feel ashamed about going to the doctor when she felt sick. She should have been in here weeks ago.

Dr. Vindaman came in, a short woman with a black braid and a brisk manner.

"Hi, Dr. Vindaman. Did they check my hormone levels?" Ronnie asked. "I wondered if it could be premature menopause. The symptoms seemed consistent."

Dr. Vindaman frowned. "Someone has been doing some amateur medical research online, eh?"

Veronica shrugged. "In my own defense, I do know quite a bit about human biology."

"I don't doubt it," Dr. Vindaman said. "My twin girls love your show. Is there going to be a new season?"

"That's up in the air," Ronnie told her. "I had a falling-out with the production company, so I'm not sure where it's going to end up."

"Well, that is a shame. Lie down on the cot. I'm going to do an abdominal ultrasound."

"Ultrasound?" Ronnie was startled. "Is something wrong?"

"Don't worry," Dr. Vindaman soothed. "Just ruling things out. Go on. Lie back and expose your lower abdomen for me."

In a few minutes, the ticklish wand was sliding through the thick, viscous goo all over her belly, but the monitor was turned to an angle where Ronnie could not see it.

After a few moments of this, she was ready to snap. "Dr. Vindaman," she pleaded. "Throw me a bone. What are you looking for?"

The doctor didn't answer for a long moment. The machine clickety-clicked as she took picture after picture. "One moment," she said, her voice abstracted. "Hang on."

Finally, she turned to Ronnie and swiveled the monitor so that she could see it. "Take a look," she said. "I think we can safely rule out premature menopause."

Ronnie looked at the screen, and her jaw dropped. Oh. *God.*

The image morphed and shifted according to how the doctor was moving the wand, but Ronnie had seen enough of her friends' sonograms to recognize what she was looking at. Which was to say…a total readjustment of her entire existence.

Her vision went dark for an instant.

"Look here," Dr. Vindaman said. "There's the head, the arms, the legs, spine. Too early to tell the sex. Another couple weeks. If you want to know, of course."

"But…but…I'm on the pill." Her voice was a thin thread of sound.

"Yes, I know." The doctor's tone was ironic. "I prescribed it for you. Were you taking antibiotics? Did you maybe forget a day, or two days?"

She thought about it. "I had an upset stomach on the day that my aunt had the heart attack. I threw up after taking the pill. I couldn't keep anything down the next day, either."

"Was that approximately sixteen weeks ago?"

"Yes," she said.

"Well, then. That was it." Dr. Vindaman looked concerned. "Is it a bad time?"

"Uh…well, I'm very surprised," she said. "Unprepared. I don't have a partner. I broke up with the man I was seeing. I certainly don't want to co-parent with him."

"I see." The doctor's voice was gentle. "So you've got some big decisions ahead. Take a couple days. Talk to your family. You can get dressed."

Ronnie thanked the doctor and said goodbye like an automaton. She didn't remember the drive home, or walking into her own condo. Time lost all meaning as she sat in the dining room, hours crawling by. Rain trickled down the window that looked out over the waterfront. There was a cup of peppermint tea in front of her, long since gone cold. The only thing her roiling stomach could stand.

She was stupefied. A baby. Wes's baby.

Her mind raced around in circles. Images, memories, feelings. Longing for what might have been. What should have been. A tornado of emotions. After it passed, her face and throat ached, but a strong, clear certainty had risen up inside her.

She wanted this baby. That both thrilled and energized her.

But what about Wes? It wouldn't stay secret. People noticed her, photographed her, wrote about her. Her pregnancy would be remarked upon. Wes would do the math.

He would want to know his own child. And as angry as she felt, she did not want to deprive her child of a father. She'd grown up without a mother. She wouldn't wish that on anyone. Still, interacting with him was going to be so awkward, considering that she missed him so badly, she hadn't been able to breathe for four months. Everything reminded her of him. Everything hurt. And now, she would have the ultimate in reminders. For the rest of her natural life.

Out of nowhere, she felt a sensation that could almost be described as hunger, rather than nausea. It had been so long, she barely recognized it.

She had to figure out how to nourish herself and this baby. She got to work, and sat down to a turkey sandwich on toast. She'd gotten through more than half of it when her smartphone buzzed. Elliott's name was on the display. She set the sandwich down.

"Hey, Elliott. What's up?"

"Um…your showbiz career?" Elliott's voice vibrated with excitement. "That's what's up, love! Things are turning around at last, and it is about time!"

"Excuse me?" she said. "What on earth are you talking about?"

"Avery got a call," Elliott said. "From Orion's Eye. It's a new streaming service. They just got a massive infusion of cash from a venture capitalist, and his only stipulation was that they produce *The Secret Life of Cells*!"

"What venture capitalist?"

"I don't know," Elliott said. "Do we care? Is it relevant? Whoever he is, I want to kiss him right on the mouth!"

"But Elliott, we can't take it to another platform," Ronnie reminded him. "Fadden Boyle will never let us out of that contract clause. We've been through this before. We have to rebrand and start from scratch, and even then, it will be tricky."

"And that, my love, is where you are dead wrong! They're letting us go!"

"Huh?" She jerked up in her chair, startled. "Really? What happened?"

"I was hoping you'd tell me. Jane said that Jareth told her we were free to take the show elsewhere. Then he told her to, and I quote, 'Tell Ronnie to call off the dogs.'"

Ronnie gasped, as realization hit. "Oh, my God!"

"So you do know!" Elliott crowed. "You've been holding out on me! Do tell!"

"Sorry, can't right now. We'll talk soon. Thanks for giving me the news."

Ronnie set the phone on the table, freshly rattled. What the hell…?

Slowly, she picked up the phone and pulled Wes's number from her contact list. Silently pleading with her heart to slow down before she hit Call.

Wes picked up swiftly. "Ronnie?"

"Hi, Wes," she said.

He was silent for a long moment. "It's good to hear your voice," he said.

Oh, God, it was good to hear his voice, too. It was beautiful. She cleared her throat. "So I heard that a mysterious venture capitalist has been prodding Orion's Eye to produce Season Four of *The Secret Life of Cells*."

"Yeah? Smart guy. Excellent investment."

"I also heard from Jareth's production company. They're letting us have the show back. And Jareth says, 'Call off the dogs.'"

"Did he?" Wes laughed under his breath. "And of course, you thought of me."

"What did you do to him? I told you to leave him alone."

"It pissed me off that he was sitting on your beautiful show like a spiteful toad," Wes said. "So I reminded him of the video I made. Remember when he threatened to destroy your career? I told him I'd send that video to some famous influencers, bloggers, vloggers, podcasters. I'm friendly with all of them, and they would make his life hell. It's not like I hit him, or anything entertaining like that."

She was struggling not to smile. Damn the man. "Wes, I can fight my own battles."

"Okay. Won't happen again. I would have run the idea past you, if you'd been speaking to me. But you weren't returning my emails or my texts, so I was forced to make decisions without guidance. We all have our limits."

Ronnie stifled a snort of laughter, and then thought of the baby. She had to tell him. But not on the phone. "Anyhow," she said. "Thanks for doing that for me."

"I wasn't doing you any favors. *The Secret Life of Cells* is an incredible property. I was just taking advantage of inside info about an amazing opportunity. So don't thank me. I'm going to make money off that move. So are you, incidentally."

"Well," she said. "Okay. Fine. Even so. Thanks, just the same."

"Whatever," he said. "Can I come over? I really want to talk."

"Wes…I don't think that I can—"

"I have your mom's baby box. Are you at home? I could come over now."

Panic stabbed through her. She couldn't. Not today, with her mind still blown from this momentous news, her eyes red and swollen, in such a vulnerable state. No way. The idea of holding his baby in her arms… Oh God.

"Not today," she said, her voice choked. "Not here."

"I'll be a perfect gentleman," he said. "The divorce

was finalized a month ago. You have no agenda, I have no agenda. All I want is to talk to you. Please, Ronnie."

Ronnie pondered that as she walked around the kitchen. It was true; they had to talk. But not at her place, and not all alone. She missed him too damn much. She might disgrace herself.

She needed her angry, indignant family around her, to make her strong. Keep her honest.

"Not at my place. Aunt Elaine's. Tomorrow. The family will all be there for lunch."

Wes made a noncommittal sound. "Your aunt won't be thrilled to see me."

"Probably not, but you'll both live," Ronnie said. "Everyone will live. Come there tomorrow at noon, if you want to talk to me. Goodbye, Wes."

She put the phone down, and stared at her own reflection in the window, her hand on her belly. Trying not to imagine, or hope, for some scenario where they could be together. She'd worked so hard to let it all go, and just the sound of his voice knocked her back to square one.

She breathed down the butterflies, which were going nuts, and suddenly, she felt it. Like the butterflies, but deeper. A delicate, ticklish flutter deep and low inside her. That wasn't nervous knots. That was a tiny live being, for which she was entirely responsible. It was miraculous, beautiful. Terrifying.

She sat and ate the rest of her sandwich. Every last bite.

Nineteen

Lizette answered the front door of Elaine Moss's mansion, at twelve on the dot. Her face was tight-lipped. Entirely different from the smiling woman who had served him her shortbread cookies just a few short months ago.

He walked in, waiting by the door. "Where shall I put Ronnie's box?"

"On the chest by the wall," Lizette instructed coldly. "Follow me, please."

She led him into the first large salon. Two people were in there. Marcus Moss, and his wife, Eve Seaton. Eve was a brunette with long, glossy curls, and Marcus Moss was even taller than Wes. Black hair, chiseled features. Biracial, the rumor mill said. Half-Asian. His mouth was tight with anger. Eve studied him coldly, arms crossed.

"This is the guy?" Marcus asked Lizette.

"Yep, he's the one," she said crisply.

"You have a lot of damn nerve, coming here," Marcus said to him.

Wes was stoic. "Ronnie said to come. I'd go to the gates of hell if she told me to."

"I'll drop kick you right through the gates of hell if you upset her," Marcus said.

Huh. His very presence would probably upset her. But after losing Ronnie, the gates of hell held no terror for him, and her family's anger was the least of his problems.

All the Mosses were trickling in, for his or her own chance to give him the fisheye. There was Tilda, and Annika, a beautiful little girl with long dark hair who ducked and wove between the older Mosses to get to the front. Annika glared at him. "Is this the guy who was mean to Aunt Ronnie?"

"Annika, go to the dining room," Tilda said.

"If you're mean to Ronnie, I'll kick your butt," Annika warned him.

"You will do no such thing, young lady," Tilda said. "Go straight upstairs."

Caleb appeared in the doorway, then Jack, with Maddie behind him. She was visibly pregnant, and as radiantly pretty as ever, but he got no smiles from her this time.

Whoa. That was a whole lot of glacial hostility to process.

"He's here?" Elaine Moss's imperious voice, behind them. "Excellent. Get out of my way, all of you. Let me get a look at him."

Elaine sailed through them in her wheelchair like the parting of the Red Sea. Her piercing gaze seemed less hostile than that of her younger relatives.

"Hello, Mrs. Moss," he said. "I'm glad to see you looking better."

"No thanks to you," Elaine said crisply.

He just waited, trying not to break eye contact. In fact, she did look pretty good, considering. Thin and pale, but her white hair stuck straight up with its usual vigor, and her eyes were sharp, studying him hard. She held an ebony cane across her lap.

"Marcus is right," Elaine said. "Coming to this house, knowing that all of us would spit in your eye, that does take nerve. I always did like that quality in a man."

"Gran!" Caleb sounded shocked. "What the hell are you saying?"

"Shush," Elaine said. "Young man, behave yourself with Ronnie, or we will destroy you. And if there's any butt-kicking to be done, I will be the one doing it." She lifted her cane, shaking it. "Don't think I'm just some helpless invalid. Clear?"

"As crystal, ma'am," he said.

Elaine harrumphed. "All right, then. She's in the library." When he didn't jump to it, she made an impatient sound. "What are you waiting for? You know the way. Go on."

He made haste to obey, passionately relieved to get the hell out of there, while at the same time, paradoxically glad that Ronnie had their fierce, unwavering support. They were a steady and dependable resource for her. He wished that he had family like that.

Then again. There was always a downside. Like that marriage mandate, for instance. Hey, he might be a loner, but he'd been spared a lot of drama. Trade-offs.

He slowed at the door to the library. *Do it, Brody.* He shoved the heavy, intricately carved wooden door open.

Ronnie was silhouetted against the window. She wore slim black pants and a long, textured sweater made of every shade of green. "Hello, Ronnie," he said.

She turned, and it cut him to the heart how beautiful she was. Too pale. Her brilliant blue eyes had smudgy shadows under them.

"Wes," she said. "Did my family behave themselves?"

"As well as could be expected," he said. "Not too terrible."

The silence was painful. There was so much he was desperate to say, but she would never accept it. He cleared his throat. "Your mom's baby box. Lizette said to leave it in the foyer."

"Thank you," she said. "I'm glad to have it back. It's precious to me."

"I was pleased to see your aunt in fighting form," he offered. "She threatened to kick my ass if I misbehaved. As did Annika. And Marcus."

Another ghost of a smile. "They are silly and over-protective."

"As well they should be," he said. "Not silly at all. I'm glad they look out for you."

"So, Wes. I appreciate your help bringing us to the attention of the Orion's Eye platform. And for prying our intellectual property free of Boyle Fadden's contract, even if your tactics were those of a Mafia don. My team is over the moon."

"I told you, it wasn't a favor. I only—"

"Yes, yes, I know. Just a business move, completely self-interested, yada yada. But still. Thanks."

"You're welcome."

"What else did you need to say to me, Wes?" she asked. "Because this is really hard."

He nodded. "I know, but I just have to say it. I love you. Always will. I can't stop thinking about you. I can't let go of the idea of being with you forever."

Her mouth shook. "Wes, don't. I'm sorry, but…don't."

His heart sank. "Absolutely never? That's still your position?"

"I see your point of view," she said. "I know that seeing your father's memory desecrated drove you to act the way you did. If I were in your position, I might have done exactly the same thing."

"I'm glad you understand," he said cautiously.

"Yes," she said. "But if I'd done what you did, the price would be the same. It would just be me paying it, instead of you. It's not for free."

"I see," he ground out.

"It hurts too much, that all those wonderful memories I have were never real. On some level, it was all just theater for you."

"No, Ronnie. It was the realest thing I've ever felt. It knocked me on my ass."

"You know I have feelings for you," she said. "But what happened left me raw inside. Everything hurts. I'm just one big walking flinch. I don't know how I could trust you again. It's not from lack of wanting to. It's because I can't."

The hope that he'd tried to keep hidden even from himself abruptly deflated, leaving him feeling empty and flat. "I understand," he said dully.

"But I have something important to tell you," she said.

Wes waited, and waited some more, vaguely alarmed. "What?" he demanded. "Is something wrong? Is everything okay with you?"

"I'm fine, but there's a new development," she said.

He guessed it, all at once, and felt like the floor had just dropped out beneath his feet. "No way."

She nodded, putting her hand on her belly.

He gasped for breath. "Holy shit, Ronnie."

She reached into a big pocket in the front of her sweater and held out a small sheaf of ultrasound photographs. "Four months," she said. "The day of Aunt Elaine's surgery. I threw up that morning, after I took the pill. The next day, I was so miserable, I couldn't keep anything down. That did the trick."

Wes took the scraps of paper and studied them. Minutes ticked by.

He struggled to speak normally. "I take it you want to keep this baby?"

"Yes," she said quietly. "Absolutely."

"Does your family know?"

"Not yet," she said. "I found out yesterday."

"I want to know my child," Wes told her.

"I figured that you would."

"So you agree to let me participate? You won't try to cut me out?"

Her hair swung forward to hide her face. "We'll… we'll work something out."

The emotional charge made it impossible to look at her, so he turned away, just to look at something else, anything else. As chance would have it, he found himself gazing at the portrait of Naomi Moss. He did not allow himself to flinch. Just looked straight at the remarkable portrait.

"It's incredible how you resemble her," he said.

Ronnie walked over to him and looked up at the portrait. "I'm glad it survived," she said. "It chills me to think how close Dad came to burning it when the shipment arrived. Aunt Elaine said the only thing that slowed him down was how big and bulky it was. He didn't have an ax handy to chop it up and feed it into the fireplace. That gave Aunt Elaine and Uncle Bertram a window of opportunity to spirit it away."

Wes looked at her. "When the shipment arrived?" he said.

"Mom's things, from Sri Lanka. Elaine told me the story when she was recuperating, in the hospital. Brushes with death make you reflect on the past, evidently."

Hairs prickled up on his neck. "This painting was in that container?" he repeated. "The one that came from Sri Lanka, after the bombing?"

"Yes. It's an Aaron Holmes. He was the hot portraitist at the time. He was vacationing there. Dad made him an offer he couldn't refuse. Dad's small superpower."

Well, hell. Wes stared up at the gleam of sly humor in Naomi Moss's blue eyes. Her expression seemed to say, *Seriously? You still don't get it?*

Of course, it no longer mattered if he got it or not. He couldn't act on it now.

But Ronnie plucked that right out of the airwaves. "What is it?" she demanded. "What are you thinking?"

Wes gestured at the portrait. "What do you think, Ronnie? Knowing me?"

Ronnie's eyes widened. "For real? You're thinking that Mom hid the documentation in her portrait? That's so cloak-and-dagger. Only you, Wes."

"I know, but it's the last place to look." He shrugged. "If you don't want to, well, tough. Too bad for me. I'll always wonder, but that's my cross to bear."

Ronnie stared up at her mother's portrait. "There's no reason for me not to check it out," she said.

His heart thudded. "No?" he asked. "Really?"

"Not for you," she said. "For me. For us. If Mom put anything in there, it wouldn't be anything she was ashamed of. It would be exactly the opposite."

"Your call," he said. "I learned my lesson. Naomi is not for me to mess with, or look at, or even like."

Ronnie reached up to seize the portrait. "All things considered, maybe I'd better look into this thing pre-emptively," she said. "Or God knows what scheme you'll come up with to get your paws on it."

He let out a rusty laugh as he helped her lift it down, turning it so that the portrait side was to the wall, and pulled his out his pocketknife. "Do you think I'll try to seduce your Aunt Elaine to get the run of the house?"

"Do not flatter yourself, Mr. Brody. You're not my type."

They turned, startled, to see Aunt Elaine being pushed through the library door by Jerome. He looked outraged when he saw the portrait off the wall.

"What are you doing?" he demanded. "Put that back where it was!"

"Wes thinks that Mom might have stored information in it," Ronnie said.

"You're letting yourself be manipulated by that bastard?" Jerome roared.

"There's no reason not to check," Ronnie said. She looked at Wes. "Go on."

Wes started gently loosening the nails that held the canvas to the frame.

"I can't believe this!" Jerome bellowed. "It's insane! I won't allow it!"

"Jerome, shut up, for God's sake," Elaine snapped. "Let's see what happens. Go on, then. Proceed."

Wes pried the frame loose of the canvas, taking care not to damage it. He lifted the canvas free of the frame and turned it around. There was a square of cardboard backing behind it, once white, now yellowed. A manila envelope was taped to it, and three letter-size envelopes. One was addressed to Jerome, one to Ronnie, and one to Elaine and Bertram.

Wes set the piece of cardboard backing on the table and stepped back to let Ronnie do the honors. Ronnie's cousins had made their way into the library and were crowded around watching. The room was hushed. Even Annika was quiet, eyes big and worried, sensing the gravity of the moment.

Ronnie detached the large envelope, and the three letters. She opened the manila envelope and looked inside. "It's full of floppy disks," she said. "Does anybody know someone with equipment that can read a format this old?"

"Give them to me," Maddie said. "I'll get right on it."

Ronnie gave the envelope to Maddie, then passed Elaine her letter, and Jerome his. Jerome's face looked stricken. He held it by his fingertips, as if it might bite him.

Ronnie settled on Elaine's wingback chair and opened her letter.

Twenty

She was intensely aware of everyone watching. Only Wes had turned his face politely away. The handwriting of her letter was different than other examples she'd seen of her mother's handwriting. Not cursive, printed much larger. Meant to be read by her seven-year-old self. Her eyes began to blur almost instantly as she read it.

Dearest Ronnie,
Sweetheart, if you're reading this, it's because the saddest thing has happened, and I won't be coming home.

I hope you never see this. I hope you see me instead. I'll hug you and kiss you, and someday, when you're grown up, I'll tell you how scared I was, and we'll laugh about it.

But just in case, I'll tell you right now that I love

*you. I'll never stop. Wherever I am in the universe,
I'll be blessing you forever.*

*I know this will be hard for Daddy. Try to be
strong if he gets sad. I sent a letter to Aunt Elaine
and Uncle Bertram, and another one to Daddy,
telling them everything that happened. They'll ex-
plain it to you when you're bigger.*

*I wish you love, baby. Be bold. Don't let real
love slip away. Try to forgive. It's always worth
the effort.*

*I love you to the ends of the known universe
and beyond.*

*All my love,
Mommy.*

She could hear her mother's voice. Her heart felt like
it would burst.

"Her letter lays it all out." Elaine's voice quavered. "It
was Raimund. The payoffs, the corruption, the cover-up,
the falsified data. Probably the bomb, as well."

"Who is Raimund?" Ronnie asked.

"Raimund Oswalt, our chief operating officer back
then," Elaine said. "Naomi says, *'Tomorrow I'm meeting
John Padraig and giving him copies of the data, just in
case. I confronted Raimund yesterday, and someone cut
the brake line of my car, which I then drove into a ditch.
I'm afraid to talk to anyone but Padraig. If anything happens to me, ask Padraig for the real story. The data is in
the floppy disks.'"* Her hands, holding the letter, dropped
to her lap. "Oh, Naomi," she whispered. "Oh, honey."

"Where is this Raimund Oswalt?" Wes asked.

"Dead," her father said flatly. "He died of cancer five

years ago. So I can't even crush him for killing my wife. He's out of my reach. Goddamn him."

Ronnie turned to her father, shocked by his eyes. He looked as if he'd been mortally wounded. "Dad?" she whispered. "Are you all right?"

"No. Raimund told me she was having an affair with Padraig. And I believed him. I paid him a fat salary and bonuses, year after year. After he killed my Naomi."

"Oh, Dad," Ronnie said. "I'm so sorry."

"I let her down," he said brokenly. "I let you down, too, Veronica. I've always let you down."

She couldn't in all honesty tell him that it wasn't true, but her heart had been softened by Mom's letter. "Maybe, before," she said. "But we can start from where we are now. We can try again and do better. Right? That's what Mom would have wanted."

Her dad nodded jerkily and covered his face with his hand.

Ronnie stared down at her letter. It was blistered with her tears.

Don't let real love slip away, Mom had said. Was that what she was doing? Was that why it felt so wrong? There had been so much pain and misunderstanding. Mom's messages of love, hidden almost in plain sight for twenty-three years, had never quite reached them… until now.

She didn't want to choose pride over love. God knows, she should have learned her lesson by now.

Elaine stood, leaning on the ebony cane. "It would seem, Mr. Brody, that we owe you an apology," she announced. "To your parents, as well, God rest their souls. On behalf of MossTech, and everyone involved, I am deeply sorry."

Wes inclined his head. "Thank you," he said. "I accept your apology. And now, if you'll excuse me, I will be on my way."

Panic exploded inside of Ronnie. "You're going now?" She felt almost frantic. "Right now? When we've finally figured it all out?"

Wes gestured at the dismantled painting, the scattered envelopes, her aunt, crying into a handkerchief, her father, who had turned away, hunched and shaking.

"It's time, babe," he said gently. "Look around yourself. The place is trashed, everyone's in turmoil. My work here is done."

"Oh, stop," she said sharply. "Don't joke about this."

"I'm in no mood to joke," he said. "This is huge, Ronnie. We proved that our parents were exactly what we believed them to be. Not crooks, but good, solid people, loving their families, doing their jobs to the best of their ability. I call that a win. I'm not going to get greedy. We'll be in touch about that…ah…that other thing we mentioned." He backed toward the door, giving her a sad, crooked little smile.

"Don't go!" She grabbed his wrist, hearing her mother's voice in her head.

Don't let real love slip away. Try to forgive. It's always worth the effort.

"Don't go," she said again, fingers clamped around his wrist.

Wes turned to look at her. "Why?" he asked quietly. "Why should I stay?"

"Because…because things are different now. Everything's changed."

"Has it?" His eyes met hers, clear and challenging. "How so?"

"My mom told me in her letter to be bold," she said. "She said not to let love slip away. To try to forgive. It's good advice, and I'm taking it. I think that she brought us together. She wanted me to be happy. I want to be happy. And you make me happy."

Joy lit up in his eyes. "I do?"

"Yes," she said forcefully. "Yes, like nothing else in the world. I love you. I want you. I'll be bold, like she said. I want this. I want to give to you and take from you and just be with you. Do you promise me that you won't lie to me? Ever again?"

"Never," Wes said fiercely. "I never wanted to. It hurt, to lie to you. Never again. I swear it."

"Good," she said. "Stay with me, then. Stay with me forever."

"Yes," he muttered, as they came together. "Oh God, yes."

They clung to each other, then Wes shifted a little. "Careful," he said softly. "We've got to watch out for the baby."

"Don't be silly," she replied. "The baby will be fine. Just hold me."

Stunned silence. "Excuse me?" Aunt Elaine said. "Did I hear you say…baby?"

Ronnie barely noticed the pandemonium that followed. She saw, heard, felt, only Wes. Her family's babbling and exclaiming could not penetrate. She wound her arms around his neck and hung on tight. At long last, her family got the hint, and cleared out of the library, all of them still talking and exclaiming. The door clicked smartly shut behind them.

Ahhh. Sweet, blessed silence.

Wes kissed her cheek, her jaw. His lips were hot and

hungry against her sensitive throat. Sweet, melting, dragging kisses. "Let's lock the door," he suggested.

She grinned, lit up with pure, incandescent happiness. "An excellent idea."

Epilogue

"That's her," the obstetrics nurse said. "Elaine Susannah Daly."

Elaine peered through the glass at her great-grandbaby, Maddie and Jack's gorgeous newborn girl. Eight pounds even, curly black hair, wiggling madly. She was the perfect baby, with her sweet little fat cheeks, and her tiny pink rosebud of a mouth.

"Oh, my goodness," she whispered. "She's so precious."

Annika jumped up and down. "Can I hold Lainie? I promise I'll be so careful!"

"All in good time, sweetheart," Elaine said, gazing raptly at the baby.

The rest of them crowded around, gazing at Lainie with soft eyes. Wes and Ronnie were there, Marcus and Eve, Caleb and Tilda and Annika. The sight of them all together made her heart thud in her chest. What a wild gamble she'd made. At the end, she'd lost, but in the great balance of things, in the long run, she'd won.

Still. She couldn't take the credit for the happiness and prosperity of her grandchildren and her niece. That was the result of their own courage and enterprise.

Not that she would ever, in a million years, admit such a thing to them.

"Elaine. Congratulations. Your family line continues."

It was Jerome's cool, dragging voice behind her. Elaine braced herself out of habit, but Jerome wasn't quite as abrasive as he used to be. Not since that trip that he and Caleb had taken to Sri Lanka, to meet with the relatives of the victims of the toxic-mold disaster.

They were in the process of making what reparations they could. That process had been very good for Jerome's general mood.

"Congratulations to you, too, Jerome," Elaine said. "You're next."

He snorted. "So are you satisfied with the result of your machinations?"

"I paid for it," she admitted. "But it was worth it. Just look at her." She gestured at the baby, and then at the rest of her family. "Aren't they a sight to behold? Our new generation. Babies, tumbling all around us in a few months."

"It'll be noisy and chaotic," Jerome observed. "You even managed to get Veronica married and pregnant. Your plotting and scheming knows no bounds."

"The timing wasn't ideal." Elaine tried not to sound bitter. "Reconciling a month after the divorce, and re-marrying in another Elvis chapel in Vegas? Good God."

"At least she invited us the second time around," Jerome observed. "Ridiculous affair."

"True, but we had fun," Elaine said. "You know what, Jerome? All in all, I'm satisfied. Even if I lost MossTech to you, I'm fine. We're all fine."

"Yes," Jerome said. "I agree. We're fine."

"Of course you're fine." Elaine's voice was wry. "You got MossTech."

"About that," Jerome said. "I thought about it, in Sri Lanka, and I've come to a decision."

"What decision?" she asked. "You are going public, of course?"

Jerome gazed at the baby. "No," he said. "I've transferred my shares of MossTech to the kids. Equally. They'll be the caretakers of MossTech's legacy now."

Elaine stared at him, open-mouthed.

"Dad," Ronnie said. "Are you serious?"

"When have I ever joked?" he asked. "Naomi gave me good advice in her letter. Twenty-three years late, but still good. She told me I had a good family, and that I should trust them. She was right. So that's what I'll do."

Wes and Ronnie exchanged startled glances. "Dad. That's…incredible."

"Besides," Jerome went on, his voice dour. "I'll be a grandfather soon, and I'm sure that will take up a considerable amount of my time and attention."

Wes's face froze in stark alarm at that prospect, but Ronnie seized her father in a fierce hug, pressing a kiss to his lean, seamed cheek. "Thanks, Dad."

"I won't be any good at it, you know," Jerome warned her. "Grandfathering, I mean. You know me. I'm impatient and bad-tempered. And stiff as a board."

"Nonsense," Elaine said briskly. "As long as you're making an effort, you'll do fine. You'll learn."

She and Jerome looked around the room. Maddie was with Jack in the recovery room, but Caleb was there with Tilda, whose belly was starting to show, and Marcus with Eve, and Ronnie and Wes, and her beautiful Annika. Her precious treasures. So lovely.

"Quite the harvest," Jerome said, in an undertone just for her ears. "Better than we deserve, eh? After all our shenanigans."

Elaine smiled. "Probably, but what the hell. We'll take it and run with it."

* * * * *

Don't miss a single story in the
Dynasties: Tech Tycoons series

Their Marriage Bargain
The Marriage Mandate
How to Marry a Bad Boy
Married by Midnight

#2911 ONE CHRISTMAS NIGHT
Texas Cattleman's Club: Ranchers and Rivals
by Jules Bennett
Ryan Carter and Morgan Grandin usually fight like cats and dogs—until one fateful night at a Texas Cattleman's Club masquerade ball. Now will an unexpected pregnancy make these hot-and-heavy enemies permanent lovers?

#2912 MOST ELIGIBLE COWBOY
Devil's Bluffs • by Stacey Kennedy
Brokenhearted journalist Adeline Harlow is supposed to write an exposé on Colter Ward, Texas's Sexiest Bachelor, *not* fall into bed with him enthusiastically and repeatedly! If only it's enough to break their no-love-allowed rule for a second chance at happiness...

#2913 A VALENTINE FOR CHRISTMAS
Valentine Vineyards • by Reese Ryan
Prodigal son Julian Brandon begrudgingly returns home to fulfill a promise. Making peace with his troubled past and falling for sophisticated older woman Chandra Valentine aren't part of the plan. But what is it they say about best-laid plans...?

#2914 WORK-LOVE BALANCE
Blackwells of New York • by Nicki Night
When gorgeous TV producer Jordan Chambers offers Ivy Blackwell the chance of a lifetime, the celebrated heiress and social media influencer wonders if she can handle his tempting offer...and the passion that sizzles between them!

#2915 TWO RIVALS, ONE BED
The Eddington Heirs • by Zuri Day
Stakes can't get much higher for attorneys Maeve Eddington and Victor Cortez in the courtroom...or in the bedroom. With family fortunes on the line, these rivals will go to any lengths to win. But what if love is the ultimate prize?

#2916 BILLIONAIRE MAKEOVER
The Image Project • by Katherine Garbera
When PR whiz Olive Hayes transforms scruff CEO Dante Russo into the industry's sexiest bachelor, she realizes she's equally vulnerable to his charms. But is she falling for her new creation or the man underneath the makeover?

*Thanks to violinist Megan Han's one-night fling with her
father's new CFO, Daniel Pak, she's pregnant! No one
can know the truth—especially not her matchmaking
dad, who'd demand marriage. If only her commitment-
phobic not-so-ex lover would open his heart…*

Read on for a sneak peek at
One Night Only
by Jayci Lee.

The sway of Megan's hips mesmerized him as she glided
down the walkway ahead of him. He caught up with her
in three long strides and placed his hand on her lower
back. His nostrils flared as he caught a whiff of her sweet
floral scent, and reason slipped out of his mind.

He had been determined to keep his distance since
the night she came over to his place. He didn't want to
betray Mr. Han's trust further. And it wouldn't be easy
for Megan to keep another secret from her father. The
last thing he wanted was to add to her already full plate.
But when he saw her standing in the garden tonight—a
vision in her flowing red dress—he knew he would crawl
through burning coal to have her again.

She reached for his hand, and he threaded his fingers through hers, and she pulled them into a shadowy alcove and pressed her back against the wall. He placed his hands on either side of her head and stared at her face until his eyes adjusted to the dark. He sucked in a sharp breath when she slid her palms over his chest and wrapped her arms around his neck.

"I don't want to burden you with another secret to keep from your father." He held himself in check even as desire pumped through his veins.

"I think fighting this attraction between us is the bigger burden," she whispered. His head dipped toward her of its own volition, and she wet her lips. "What are you doing, Daniel?"

"Surviving," he said, his voice a low growl. "Because I can't live through another night without having you."

She smiled then—a sensual, triumphant smile—and he was lost.

Don't miss what happens next in…
One Night Only
by Jayci Lee.

Available December 2022 wherever
Harlequin Desire books and ebooks are sold.

Harlequin.com

HDEXP1022

Love Harlequin romance?

DISCOVER.

Be the first to find out about promotions,
news and exclusive content!

Facebook.com/HarlequinBooks

Twitter.com/HarlequinBooks

Instagram.com/HarlequinBooks

Pinterest.com/HarlequinBooks

YouTube.com/HarlequinBooks

ReaderService.com

EXPLORE.

Sign up for the Harlequin e-newsletter and
download a free book from any series at
TryHarlequin.com

CONNECT.

Join our Harlequin community to
share your thoughts and connect
with other romance readers!
Facebook.com/groups/HarlequinConnection

HARLEQUIN

Heartfelt or thrilling, passionate or uplifting—Harlequin is more than just happily-ever-after.

With twelve different series to choose from and new books available every month, you are sure to find stories that will move you, uplift you, inspire and delight you.

SIGN UP FOR THE HARLEQUIN NEWSLETTER

Be the first to hear about great new reads and exciting offers!

Harlequin.com/newsletters

HNEWS2021